THE PETER PAN
SYNDROME

THE PETER PAN SYNDROME

SYNDROME

Gillian Lyden

To order additional copies of this book, contact:
Xlibris Corporation
0-800-644-6988
www.xlibrispublishing.co.uk
orders@xlibrispublishing.co.uk
300015

PART ONE

The city was hot and stuffy—no air-conditioning in the streets between the ever burgeoning buildings. Probably irritated by the heat in the airless streets the children were marching for the third time that year. Banners flapped above their heads. **"THE TIME IS NOW!" and RIGHTS FOR CHILDREN!"** and the longest:-

"WE WANT WORK NOT PLAY—LET US GROW UP TODAY!"

"I wonder what started them off this time Sir?" The Minister for Subject Monitoring (applied to both people and paperwork!) addressed his superior, whose bull neck and craggy jaw belied the well-coiffured blonde waves adorning his head. The steely-blue eyes narrowed as he responded, "I don't know, but I think you'll agree it is not going to go away—we have to do something about it". The Head of Combined Affairs (H.C.A.) Jack Bailey, was running out of patience. "What are your plans Minister?"

"Everything is under control, Sir." Jim knew better than to address his boss as 'Jack' when he was in a mood like this. "We are going to operate the automatic street cleaners if they don't respond to our requests." There was a short silence as the Head evaluated this information. "Hmm-mm," Jim could see him stroking the waves at the back of his head as he thought, "Well. A blast of cold water up the trouser leg should cool their tempers I suppose, but if it doesn't work, and they march again before the end of the year I shan't be able shirk my responsibility. To be honest, your job is on the line Jim!" The video link was cut off.

CHAPTER 1

The sun was hot, but a chill breeze blew in off the sea, ruffled Katy Stone's blonde curls and whipped up goosebumps on her smooth, creamy skin. She shivered. Her husband, Ian, lying in a depression in the sand felt only the heat of the sun, "Cold?" he said incredulously, then noticing her hair fluttering in the breeze, "Come here and let me warm you!" He pulled her down to him and held her close, his face in the hollow of her neck, "God! How I love you!" He mumbled against her skin, feeling the same exquisite pang as on the first day he saw her on this very beach.

"I love you too," Katy laughed, "I'll never tire of you—or this beach. Do you remember—?

"Yes." their eyes met in complete and loving understanding," Can you stand another hundred years?"

"Two hundred!" laughed Katy, pulling away from him, "We'd better pack our things and leave—it's getting late."

Their children came running from the sea, scattering icy drops in a chattering shiver,

"Oo-v-v-v-v! It's freezing!" Sarah grabbed a towel, and wrapping it around her shoulders, flung herself on the sand by Ian. "Dry my back, Dad!" She began to dry her feet with a corner of the towel, sand and all.

"Wait! Get rid of the sand first." Katy leant across and poured handfuls of dry sand over Sarah's shins and feet, "M-m-mm! Nice and warm." Sarah luxuriated in the attention as she marvelled for the thousandth time how the hot, dry sand soaked up the water and left her feet dry and warm. Michael, scorning help, stood drying his hair, his body already dry. "I'm getting tired of this beach." he said truculently, his dark brows fixed in a frown, "We've been coming here for years!" Sara was pulling on her top.

"You're an old misery!" she laughed, "Always complaining!" She suddenly leapt forward and pulled at a spike of his hair. "Come on—let's look for shells and crabs in the rock pools!"

"Ouch! I'll get you for that!"

"Only five minutes, kids!" Ian shouted after them. They waved in acknowledgement and rushed towards the rocks.

Together Katy and Ian packed together the bags, towels and beach toys. "I know it's old-fashioned," Ian said, "but I do like coming to the beach like this at week-ends—it's much more invigorating than the pool with it's air-conditioning, artificial plants and predictable waves!"

"And dangerous too!" Katy smiled, looking at him knowingly. She was aware of his delight in the challenge of the natural waves. They sat down to wait for the children. Ian frowned, "I hope the march has finished by the time we get back—I don't want Michael upset again."

"Sure to have finished—don't worry, he hasn't mentioned it for weeks!" She saw the children running back from the rocks

"We might as well start climbing the cliff—they'll soon catch up with us!"

The children caught up with and passed them before they reached the top, "It's all very well for you!" shouted their father," You have nothing to carry!"

"We could have brought 'Buttle', Katy said wistfully as she struggled with the picnic things and the towels, "**he** would have carried **everything**."

"He is wonderful, but he **is** only a robot—he would probably have rolled down the bank and deprogrammed himself, then we would have had to send him back to the Centre and do without him for a week!" They halted just over the top of the cliff to catch their breath and saw the children hopping up and down with impatience by the Transporter—Government approved, re-programmable and non-disposable 'Hoverbug' ('Don't be dense! Well worth the expense!" so ran the sales pitch)—and so it had proved. Many of their friends and work colleagues had bought cheaper models and lived to regret it when they had run out of useful life in the middle of long journeys with all the embarrassment of being stuck in the mandatory Airtrac, holding up all the traffic, then being hauled off the Way by the ancient but still serviceable heliporter, dumped at Disposal and left to find their own way home!

The parking area was empty but for their Transporter—Katy thought the beach was not as popular as it ought to be. They hovered out onto the Way. As Ian touched the controls, the Autohover bug contacted the travel beam smoothly, ready to hover them effortlessly to the city. Ian breathed a sigh of relief and relaxed into the comfort of his seat, it was good to know that he could leave the journey to Programming—150 km was a long way after a day at the beach!

He passed his hand across a blue light on the instrument panel and the bug was filled with the sound of soothing music.

"Not this old stuff again!" Michael complained. "I'm fed up with being a child! I don't get to decide anything, you and Mum do it all for me."

"Oh! Not **that** again," mocked Sarah, "You should make the most of it—you can't go back once you've grown up. I think I'd like to stay a child for ever!"

"You wait until you've been a child as long as I have, Sister!" Michael wagged an aggressive finger at her. "Ninety years is a long time!"

"Don't argue kid!" Ian sat up and turned to look at Michael, "We'll talk about it at home, perhaps it is time we let you decide what you want to do." Katy's hand caught at his arm. She did not speak but the unshed tears in her eyes spoke for her. Ian placed his hand over hers and smiled at her compassionately, "The time has to come." He said quietly, then, "How about we turn the seats around and have a nice old fashioned game of bridge?" The children acquiesced eagerly as they had been learning bridge skills for some years and Michael in particular liked to beat his parents.

The arrival warning went off towards the end of the deciding game (they were one rubber all, kids against parents, having had a breaks for drinks, snacks and naps)—the kids were winning. There was a bleep from the dash-board,

"Warning call. 10 minutes to arrival at turn-off. Please access the controls." They finished the hand. The voice became more high-pitched "*Seats not adjusted: Seats not adjusted: 5 minutes to turn-off.*" Ian and Kathy quickly adjusted their seats to face forward and Ian took the wheel ready to exit the beam and take over from Airtrac just before the junction, leaving the kids to put away the cards.

Katy put her hand on his knee, "Oh! Thank goodness we had Airtrac to bring us home—you would have been exhausted driving all that way and then having to drive round the Outroad to get home." "**Exit The Way! Exit The Way! Switch to manual!**" The voiced warning panicked at Ian's finely judged manoeuvre and almost immediate slight wobble as he changed to driver control. As they hovered sedately along the City Way (it was a punishable offence to hover over any buildings as too much damage had been caused in the past) and the roads had to be used.

There was a road-block and diversion at the cross-roads, police stopping craft and directing people to turn right or left, away from the City Way. "Sorry for the inconvenience, sir. There's been a demonstration—the diversion is temporary but no craft is allowed into the city centre." Ian took the right turn.

Sailing into the Block, they saw some of the children's friends walking home in small hang-dog groups. Sarah turned to look out of the back window, "There's Jodie and Fergus! What's the matter with them?"

Michael looked out of his window, "And there's Pogie and Pam. They're soaking wet!" He wound down the window and shouted to his buddies, but their reply was lost as the car sped on. "Da-ad! You could have slowed down."

"You know Buttle will have the meal ready, and if we don't get there in time and he develops a glitch in his programming, he'll clear it away and throw it in the waste."

Katy looked at her glowering son through the mirror. "You can go round to their house later—or use the call screen."

"Okay." Michael accepted grudgingly. Buttle waited patiently in the eating area having set the table with the meal Katy had programmed, "M'mmmmm! Peking style!" Michael rushed to the table and began to help himself. "—thank Goodness Buttle had no glitches!" Katy caught at Ian's arm and gave him a warning look as he opened his mouth to complain about Michael's manners—she didn't want 'the mood' to intensify.

"Mum. What **is** 'Peking Style'?" asked Sarah. Katy hesitated and looked at Ian. "I'm not sure Sarah." Ian took over,

"Before Gene Control, Sarah—there used to be countries. One of them was called China, and that is where this kind of meal came from. Haven't you done anything about that at school?" "No Dad." Katy nudged him sharply with her elbow, and he said no more.

The fresh air had done wonders for their appetites, and in less than half an hour Katy flicked the controls at Buttle to clear away and they all trooped into the viewing room. Michael hesitated in the doorway, which slid impatiently backwards and forwards unable to shut itself. Ian beckoned to him, "Come right in Michael, please! The last thing I want to do tonight is spend two hours trying to fix the door programming".

"Yes!" Sarah said feelingly, "Last time it broke I couldn't get into the bathroom for ages and I nearly wet myself." Michael stepped in impatiently. "I don't want to view now. You said I could go and see Pogie and Fergus to find out what happened."

"Go on then—but I want you back in an hour! You have HOMEWORK!" The front door closed as Ian shouted the last word.

At Pogie and Pam's Michael pressed the viewing button by the door and a small picture of Jaimie, their mother, appeared, "Pogie's gone round to Fergus's. He said to tell you to go round if you came."

"Thanks Pam!" He ran across the grass leaping over flowers and shrubs—sometimes it felt good to be a kid he thought. Would he be able to jump so high if he were older? Right now it didn't matter, he was intent on seeing his friends. At Fergus's house Pogie and Fergus rushed out of the door wearing their flight-belts as soon as he rang.

"Where's your flight-belt?"

"I felt like running."

"Never mind. We'll give you a lift." They each put an arm around his waist and Michael put his arms around their necks. With a quick look around to make sure no-one was watching (although flight belts were programmed to fly only a foot off the ground parents disapproved of sharing—it was too easy to drop someone!) the three of them zoomed off to the play-den they had constructed in the forest. At their age the boys had plenty of experience of construction work—in history of technology they had learned to build a brick wall, footings and all—as well as log cabins. The den was wattle and daub, fitting in with revision about the Middle Ages.

In the privacy of the den they could talk freely. "What happened in the city today?" Michael asked eagerly.

"We marched again," chorused Pogie and Fergus, "it was going really well—there were lots of banners and someone had worked out this really good slogan." Fergus pulled Pogie to his feet and the two of them punched the air as they shouted,

"WE WANT WORK NOT PLAY!—LET US GROW UP TODAY!" They sat down, dejected, "And then what?" Michael urged.

"They switched on the street cleaners and raised the kerbs to thigh height—like they do for the water festival." Pogie plonked his chin in his hands miserably.

"Oh, No! No wonder you were soaking wet." Michael was angry. "Why won't they listen to us?" Fergus shrugged. There was a short silence. Then Pogie said tentatively,

"Actually, I don't know if it's a good idea to grow up. It's irreversible you know and most of the time I really enjoy hanging around with you two and just being a kid."

"Yes, me too," said Fergus.

Michael agreed, "Yes, but I want to know what it's like to do all the things that adults do. I'm fed up with being bossed around. I think I'd like kids of my own."

After another silence, Fergus looked at his buddies and dropped his bombshell. "My parents said I could go to the Gene Centre after my next birthday if I really wanted to."

Contemplating the enormity of life without Fergus silenced the other two, they looked first at each other and back at their friend. "It would be awful without you," choked Pogie, "promise you won't go without us."

"Please!" Michael begged, "Wait until our parents agree too! I always want to be friends with you and Pogie—and if you grow up without us we'll just be kids to you—you'll only want to hang around with the older boys."

"O.K. I'll wait a bit longer."

*　　*　　*

"He really means it Katy." Ian lay with his arm across her body, holding her tight. "It isn't as though we're going to lose him for ever, he'll come back and see us—and we'll still have Sarah for a while."

"You know what will happen next—Sarah will miss Michael so much that she'll want to go to the Gene Control Centre too—that's what happened with Jack and Simon."

"You know we can still have more children."

"We're only allowed two more, we've had four already."

"Don't you think we could manage with the grandchildren—or just have one child at a time instead of two?"

"I couldn't live without children—not unless we go to Gene control too—I'll still keep getting broody, and it's not really fair to have one child—it would be lonely."

"Forever young is not so easy. Perhaps we should go to the next stage—just past fertility—or perhaps we could have another fifty years seeing the world?" He peered over her shoulder questioningly.

"It would be good if we really saw the world—but we don't. All we do is visit other areas of Gene Control. They tell us there are no countries left and they're getting very suspicious about people talking about that—all they say is that we're not allowed Outside, where all the people who've left Gene Control live."

"It would be good to see where the countries used to be—you know—England; France; Thailand—Germany too—there were so many countries—Australia too!" Ian looked crestfallen, and Katy relented, "They won't let us do that! But we'll think about going abroad to other centres." She squeezed his hand, "In the mean time, perhaps you're right. Perhaps it is time for Michael to go to the next stage—puberty? If that is enough for him—some of them want to move on faster". Ian turned her face towards him and kissed the end of her nose.

"He'll have to have some time as a teenager. A sudden rush of hormones would be a disaster. Anyway, I'm pretty sure Gene Control wouldn't allow him to grow up too fast, so we'll have him on our hands for at least two years—you never know, he may like being a teenager so much he wants to stay that way for years."

Katy sat up, "Especially if we let him find a job! You were a teenager for 20 years,—until you met me!"

"Well! There you are. I don't know what you were worrying about."

*   *   *

PART TWO

Jim Speke, Minister for Subject Monitoring, walked warily into the HCA's office. "Ah! There you are Jim! His boss came out from behind the desk and proffered his hand, "Well done! You handled that superbly—that should keep them quiet for a while. I wondered if you fancied an old fashioned game of golf—they've reactivated the antique course at St. Andrews."

'—*back in favour thank God!*' thought Jim, and aloud, "That would be highly acceptable Jack."

"Have you got a golfing outfit—everybody wears the old-fashioned outfits, you know? Plus-fours, spiked shoes, golf bags—I've got outfits to spare, you can borrow one of mine. Agreed?

"Thank you, Jack."

"Right. If tomorrow suits, we'll take the shuttle tomorrow lunch time and spend the afternoon there—we'll be back in time for dinner tomorrow night."

'*that's going to cost and arm and a leg—not at my expense I hope!*' thought Jim, aloud he said, "Thank you very much, Jack. I'll bring my clubs tomorrow morning."

Chapter 2

The Call Screen sang out, "Call for Katy! Call for Katy! Call f—," Katy rushed in and turned on as she flung herself into the viewing seat. It was Pogie's Mum.

"Hi Pam. You O.K.?"

"No. I'm not. Pogie says Fergus's parents have agreed to let him go to the Gene Centre after his next birthday. Katy! They're going to let him grow up, and both of our boys are bound to want the same." Katy was silent. "Did you hear me?"

"Yes. I heard. Michael has been discontented for some time now. Ian and I were talking about it yesterday. We've almost decided to let him go to the Centre."

"But you can't—"

"Listen Jaimie. It will be O.K. They won't be allowed into adulthood straight away—if we let them get jobs it will keep them happy for a while—and we have to let them grow up some time!"

Jaimie sounded defeated and unhappy, "I suppose you're right. They'll have to be teen-agers for a while. But I don't want to lose Pogie yet—we've used up our allowance and can't have any more children."

"Ian suggested we might have a few years travelling—and after all, we'll still have the grandchildren. You'll have Pam and we'll have Sarah, and Pogie and Michael will want children of their own eventually. You'll see, the time will go quickly." Katy was trying to convince herself as much as Jaimie.

"I won't be able to stand getting broody and not being able to have any more children, and you know they haven't been able to find a cure for that without us going on to non-fertility!"

"I'm seriously considering that!" Katy could see tears rolling down Jaimie's cheeks.

"I can't bear the thought of living indefinitely and never having children again," Jaimie sobbed, "I've got to go." The screen abruptly went blank. Katy switched off the screen with a worried look on her face. *'Poor Jaimie'*, she thought, *'I know how she feels.'*

The door slid open and Ian came in, "What's up Honey?" he said as he joined her in the viewing seat and swept her into his arms.

"It's Jaimie. She says Fergus's parents are allowing him to go to Gene Control after his next birthday."

"What's the problem with that"

"Our boys are going to want to go with him—you know—they've been inseparable for years, and if one opts to grow older they'll want to stick together. It won't be so much fun without their friend."

"I suppose you're right." He smoothed her hair with his lips, smelling the familiar sweetness of her. "It wasn't much fun when my friends went up into puberty, we had nothing in common after that. But I stayed where I was for my Mum's sake. As you know, Dad had left her for someone else when I was a baby and she never found anyone else. After 20 years at Puberty level when I met you and went on to adulthood, she joined the Campaigners for Natural Aging and went Outside. I don't know if she's still alive."

"And we can't find out without joining her and cutting ourselves off from civilisation for ever. The Gene Centre will never allow us back in." Ian huffed, "Huh! Neither will they let us out!"

They sat in silent communion for some minutes. Katy spoke again, "You know there's something peaceful; a sense of release to think of letting life take it's natural course."

"Mmmm . . ." Ian was still kissing her hair. "—but don't let the Authorities hear you say that! Are you bored with our life, Katy?"

"Never! But then we were so very lucky to find soul-mates in each other. I will love you forever, but many people have not been so fortunate. A hundred years is a terribly long time to be alone." The door slid open with an urgent 'whoosh!' and Michael and Sarah rushed in. Seeing their parents snug in the viewing seat they piled in on top of them. Thirty and fifty years old, or the eleven and twelve they still appeared to be, they were used to demonstrating their feelings openly, and in spite of all the knowledge they had assimilated they were still physically and emotionally pre-pubescent. "Bundle of Love!" demanded Sarah, and in two seconds was screaming with helpless laughter as Ian enclosed his family in a fiercely loving hug.

Hug over, they all flopped back into the comfortable curves of the seat, Michael next to Ian and Sarah next to Katy at either end of the seat.

"Dad?" Michael said questioningly as he looked up at his father, "Fergus is going to the Gene Centre after his next birthday—and Pogie's going to ask his parents for their permission to go too. Please, will you let me?"

"Your mother and I were just discussing this problem. We know how you feel because we've both been through that, but we haven't made a decision yet. Would you give us a little while to think about it? When is Fergus's birthday?"

"In about three weeks."

"We'll talk about it again in a week's time. You talk to Pogie and Fergus and we'll talk to their parents, then we'll try and have a family conference between all of us. Will that do?"

"Thanks Dad!" Michael gave him a hug. "Come on Sarah—let's see what Buttle will be serving for dinner!" The children left at speed.

Katy and Ian laughed, "If only it were so easy to solve these problems!" Katy said as she heaved herself out of the seat. In the event problems became more difficult than any of them could have imagined.

They had decided by the end of the week to allow Michael to go to Gene Control with his friends if their parents were also in agreement. He was over the moon, and the door system worked overtime as he careered through the house leaping and somersaulting over the furniture and ending up collapsed in the viewing seat just as screen call was activated. "Call for Anybody; Call for Anyb—" Katy strolled over as Michael activated the screen. Something red was running down the screen. Michael grimaced, "U-ugh! What's that? It's not on our side."

"Help! Michael!"

"A-A-aaaaah!" There was a loud scream, and the screen was nullified from the other side. Ian leapt from his seat in the games area where he and Katy had been practising Bridge, "What on earth was that?"

"I think it was Pogie?" Michael said, puzzled. "I'll go round and see what's the matter".

"No! You stay here." Katy grabbed him, "Stay in the games area and don't move until we come back." She gave Ian a meaningful glare over Michael's head.

"But he's my friend and—".

"Do as your mother says!" Ian's unaccustomed abruptness silenced Michael's protestations. "We'll be back shortly."

On the way out of the house Ian picked up a couple of stun guns from the storage cupboard and passed one to Katy. "What did you see?" he asked as they hurried down the block and across the grass.

"I think there was blood running down the screen in Pogie's house." Katy panted.

"When we get there, you go to the front and I'll go to the back. Give me ten seconds—it's further to the back door—then press the viewing screen so that we both press more-or-less at the same time. Then perhaps Pogie or Pam can get to one of the doors. If an adult comes out don't hesitate, put your stunner on maximum and fire—it won't do any serious harm to them and it could save you from injury." As he finished speaking they arrived at the house. Ian ran round to the back counting slowly and silently '1, ... 2, ... 3, ... 4, ... 5, ... 6, ... 7, ... 8, ... 9, ... 10—*Hope you're ready Honey!*'—He pressed the viewing button. Nothing happened for a moment, then he heard the sound of running feet and Katy came round the corner shepherding two weeping children in front of her.

"Dad's h-h-hurting Mummy!" sobbed Pam, eyes and nose dripping with tears. Pogie gasped, "There's a lot of blood—I think she'll die if nobody helps her."

"Is the back door open?" Ian gently gripped Pogie's shoulders.

"Yes," gulped Pogie.

"Take the kids to our place and phone the Authority." Ian gave Katy a quick kiss and hurried round to the back door. Inside a scene of horror greeted him—the Utility area was slippery with blood. Screams came from somewhere inside the house. He leapt over the slippery floor onto already stained carpet in the food preparation area and began to follow the screams, through the viewing lounge to the lift and up to the bedrooms. "Help me! Help me!" came Jaimie's pitiful cries.

"No-one can help you now!" Whack! "I'm not going to live forever with you!" Whack! "I've had enough of you!"

Ian walked softly into the master bedroom to see Tom with a dumb-bell lifted above his head about to bring it down on Jaimie's bleeding arms which she had folded over her head for protection. Ian had the stun gun raised in a defensive position—just at the right height to get Tom right between the eyes—he fired. Tom's arm dropped to his side, the dumb-bell dropped harmlessly to the floor and he fell pole-axed to the floor. Jaimie speechlessly lifted one blood-soaked arm towards him, the elbow bent at an impossible angle, the other fell to her side. Tucking the stun gun into his belt, he lifted her gently into his arms and carried her to the lift. As they came out into the viewing room they were faced with a barrage of stun-guns in the hands of six or seven riot police. "Halt or be shot!" Ian gently laid Jaimie on the ground and stood up with his hands raised, as a policemen rushed forward to search him he said, "I have just rescued her from her husband who is upstairs—probably recovering from stun effects—he was being extremely violent and I think you should restrain him before he comes round properly."

Seeing that Ian was completely reasonable and calm, one of the men stayed behind and helped him carry Jaimie to the waiting Meditrans outside where the medics took Jaimie into their care and flew her to the Gene Centre for repair (They *were* allowed to hover over the buildings). "You did well sir. I need to take your details—Gene Control number?" Ian gave it, "Anyone else live in this house?"

"Two children, Pam and Pogie—my wife has taken them to our house because the family are our friends and they will feel at home with us—they often sleep over."

"That will be fine for the time being, sir, but the judge may have different ideas when he adjudicates the case. Thanks for your help—we may need to ask more questions later but I'll get your address from the records at Gene Control." He turned as the other riot police came out of the house carrying Tom between them. He was securely restrained, which was just as well as he was coming round in just the same violent mood as when Ian knocked him out. He saw Ian,

"Traitor!" he bellowed, "It was you who knocked me out! Watch your back when you walk on the Block—I'll be waiting!"

"Thought you said they were your friends?" The Officer who had taken his number tucked away his recorder.

"They were! I can't understand what has happened to Tom!" They watched as Tom was loaded into the riot hover, the Officer said,

"All in the day's work, sir. Don't forget to get in touch with Police Files on your Call Screen as soon as you get home—the crime number and forensic details are on this card," he gave Ian a white card, "—just feed it into the slot and an officer will take down everything you remember. I'll see you later." He flicked the bullet-proof shield over his face and became once more an intimidating, anonymous robotic figure as he climbed into the riot cab and drove away.

Ian walked slowly home, his mind a whirl of wondering and horror. He felt as though his family's world was being turned completely upside-down, what with Michael's desire to go to Gene Control, Katy's fears about the future and the two little lost souls who waited at home with Katy and his own children. Still, the first thing was to get this report out of the way—he quickened his step. Katy welcomed him with open arms, "I've been so worried about you!" Then, whispering,—Pogie and Pam were covered in blood!"

"Where are they?" Ian hugged her reassuringly.

"I've cleaned them up and given them clothes to wear and they're with Michael and Sarah in the games room."

"I won't talk to them yet—I have to report to Police Files."

"They're not blaming you, are they? We've never had to deal with Police Files before."

Katy sounded scared, "You remember the Pitsons? No-body saw them after they reported that crime three years ago".

"I'm sure that isn't going to happen to us. I'm just going to record what happened as I remember it and view it to make sure I've remembered everything before I give it to the Files." Finally satisfied he had forgotten nothing, Ian reported to Files. The Officer recorded his statement, then the questions began. "Could you describe again the original viewing on your call screen?"

"My wife and son saw that—the screen was de-activated before I got to it—it might have been on 'record', I haven't checked."

"Check that and keep the recording if there is one. We'll need to talk to your wife and son too—tell them to prepare statements and call when they're ready." He changed the subject. "Are the two children you took home genetically related to you or your wife?"

"No, Officer."

"They'll probably have to go into Child Rescue then. Are you able to look after them for a while?"

"Of course! We've known them for forty or fifty years—they're like family to us."

"Hmmm". The officer sounded cynical and gave Ian a quizzical look from under his eyebrows. "Well, if they're not genetically related you won't be allowed to keep them. You might get visitation rights—if you're lucky!"

"You make it sound as though they're going to be in prison!"

"They'll be well fed and cared for, but it's not the Control Centre's policy to let orphans go to other families."

"But they're not orphaned—their mother is alive—at least she was the last time I saw her—so was their father!" The horror grew worse all the time.

"Mother's in intensive care and may be irreparable—there's a limit to what even Gene Control can do. As to the father—they'll probably have to rearrange a few of his genes (this is not for repeating. We're on a top security line here!) and it's anybody's guess if he'll remember the family afterwards".

Ian gasped at this unbelievable criticism of Gene Control. "Officer! I work there!" "It may seem strange to you, Sir, but as a police officer I've probably had far more experience of their results than you have. Have you not noticed the occasional disappearances of people after they've been to Gene Control?" '*this policeman is being very careless*', Ian thought for a moment, "Yes. I do know of one disappearance."

"If you ask me Sir, there's a bit too much of the 'Control' and not enough care with the gene therapy!" He seemed to relent. "If I can do anything, I will, but the most I can promise is that you can possibly keep the children until the mother is better or—." He left the unthinkable unspoken. "You realise at some time you will have to bring the children to the centre for Recall? It's not our policy to take statements from minors whilst they are conscious—it just adds to the trauma."

"Yes. Thank you Officer," Ian had forgotten the deep hypnosis sessions he had read about in the rules and regulations. *'I should have realised Pogie and Pam would have to give evidence of some kind—after all, they're the main witnesses,'* he thought.

"I'd like the other statements as soon as possible," the Officer said, "—replace the card in the slot when you're ready and I'll see you then." Ian ejected the card and left it in the holder for Kathy's later use.

The children were playing Light Battles—Ian got zapped as soon as he walked into the games room, but as he was not wearing a stun suit he was unaffected by the blue ray. Pam was lying on the floor, giggling helplessly because her suit having been zapped had temporarily stiffened—all but one arm of it—which left her waving helplessly, her Light Rayser being in the other hand. She was very like her mother and for a moment Ian was back in the other house seeing Jaimie's blood-stained hand waving beseechingly. Speechless, he finally pulled himself together, mentally thanking Heaven that children could be so resilient, and went to find Katy. Statements sent (none were taken from Pogie and Pam), boys off to the forest to find Fergus and girls up to Sarah's room to do each other's hair (Ian and Katy had decided to try to keep things as normal as possible) the adults relaxed in the viewing area.

"They probably won't think about it until bedtime," Ian said as they cuddled each other, "Then it will hit them like a ton of uranium."

"—and probably cause as much damage." said Katy, shaking her head. Buttle's alarm signalled the five-minute alarm for their evening meal and he began to make ready the eating area.

Ian called the mini view-call at the den, "You can bring Fergus to dinner if his mum allows—it's ready now."

"Thanks Dad! We're on our way!"

As Katy had foreseen, as long as the children were doing the things they normally did, they were fine, but bedtime after Fergus had gone home was traumatic. "I want Mummy," sobbed Pam.

"Mummy's in hospital, as soon as she's better you can go home."

"Why can't Dad look after us?" Pogie looked at Katy with a frown. Katy was aware that both children had the worldly wisdom to understand all this by virtue of their years of education and experience, but the emotional maturity to cope with such trauma was just not available to them. They were in complete denial of everything that had happened.

"Your Dad is not at home yet—he has to explain to the police what happened. Try not to worry, both of you, and we'll call the Control Centre tomorrow morning to find out how Mummy is. We'll look after you until everything is back to normal." Pogie and Pam flung their arms around her, "Thank you Mrs. Stone!"

"Just call me 'Katy'," she smiled at them, "and try to go to sleep."

PART THREE

The HCA was in a bad mood—Jim could tell. He had been snarling at Jim all morning. It was not until lunch time that Jim found out why, when he was called into the HCA's office. 'Jim! The problem arising today concerns your department."

"What problem is that, Sir?"

"As Minister for Subject Control, I would have expected you to know that!" snarled his boss, "Yesterday, a fellow called Tom Mailer lost control and attacked his wife—she is not expected to survive (at least, not without considerable technical input)—had you not heard about that?"

"No Sir! When did it happen?"

"Yesterday afternoon". Jim hesitated. "WELL! I'M WAITING!" Bellowed his boss.

"If you remember, Sir . . ." "YES?" "We went to play golf yesterday afternoon. I received no urgent messages when I got back—everyone had left the building except the robot guards." After a short silence, the HCA gave a small cough, "Hmmn. Well, I suppose you couldn't help that". He looked down and fiddled with things on his desk. "I'll . . . overlook it this once, but make sure you check your messages every day Jim".

"Very well Sir". *Whew! That was a close thing!* Jim went back to his office and flopped into his chair with relief. *I was nearly out of a job there!* He thought.

CHAPTER 3

The following morning at eight o'clock (amongst re-assurances to Pam and Pogie that Katy would contact the hospital about Jaimie) the children were packed off to 'Classes' as the Education Centre was known. They would be there until midday and be home for a snack about one o'clock, after which normally, the day was their own to socialise, play, help in the house or do homework. Katy would organise the house whilst they were away—programme the robots and cleaning systems (especially Buttle who had lately been rather unreliable and hurled meals into the waste-disposal because the timer had accelerated and they seemed to be late for the meal) make sure all the clothes and bedding were clean and that Central Stores were aware of their nutritional needs.

Ian would go to his job at Gene Control—checking the computers and dealing with any problems which might arise (there was not much to go wrong as the computers were self-regulating and mostly serviced and repaired themselves, but very occasionally something serious went wrong and someone had to switch over to the Backup system with the minimum delay—otherwise people undergoing genetic repair or being 'matured' could suffer irreparable genetic damage). His was a very responsible job, and the shifts were short because of the intense concentration necessary so he was usually home before the children—and ready to make sure they did their homework!

As the last of their expanded family left Katy called Gene Control to find out how Jaimie was progressing. The automatic response system informed her mechanically that Mrs. Mailer was 'progressing satisfactorily', '—thank Goodness it wasn't, *'As well as could be expected,'* thought Katy, aware that the latter message boded ill for the patient. She sank into the viewing seat with a sigh of relief. Whilst catching her breath she idly activated the screen to catch up on the news before she started work. "—and here is the scene of yesterday's tragedy where two children still in the pre-pubertal stage witnessed the savage beating of their mother by their father. We—". Katy sat up with a gasp, Pogie and Pam's home was on screen fronted by police vehicles, commentators and cameramen! "—it is understood that both parents are currently under-going treatment at Gene Control. In the immediate aftermath of this rare crime the children are temporarily with friends of the family. That is the end of the News Flash. More news at midday." Katy nullified the screen, hesitated for a few moments, then put the screen into call mode *'should I call Ian?'* she thought, *'he doesn't like me to call him at work.'* She nullified the screen again, deciding to wait until he came home. "Call for Katy; Call for Katy; Call f—". The screen re-activated, it was Janice, Fergus's mother. "Katy? Thank goodness you're in! Have you seen the news?"

"Yes, Janice."

"Whatever happened ?"

"Why don't you come over for coffee? I haven't seen you for ages—we wanted to talk to you about the boys going to Gene Control."

"Oh, well—yes. Shall I come over now or a bit later?"

"I think now would be lovely. See you in a few minutes." The screen was nullified and Katy went out to the eating area where Buttle was plugged in to Central Stores and programmed him for midday snacks and the evening meal for six. It was sometimes better to make sandwiches herself, but it looked as though it was liable to be a busy day. As she finished, the door screen buzzed and Janice's face appeared on the small screen, Katy said,

"Come in Janice." and pressed 'Door open', and '2COFFEE/MILK; 1WITH SUGAR' on Buttle's controls. They sat down in the eating area. Janice looked anxious,

"What terrible news! As if the boys aren't already mixed up enough over growing up. This is going to upset them even more. Do you know what happened? Fergus told me a little about it yesterday, but until I saw it on the news I thought he was exaggerating!" Katy said,

"I do. This is for your ears only (you can tell Bob of course)." Katy told her what had happened, then, "The children are with us, but we have been told they may have to go to Child Rescue, and I wouldn't want any child I knew to go to that soulless establishment."

Janice was silent for a moment, then quietly, "Can I confide in you Katy?" Katy nodded. Janice's eyes filled with tears and her hand covered her mouth. Katy put her arm around Janice and drew her close. "Bob and I have been thinking of—" Janice looked around fearfully, "—promise not to tell ANYONE?" Katy hugged her and nodded. "Katy—we might go Outside."

"Outside?' Katy almost shouted, "Sorry—I was just so surprised." Buttle, only his back visible, stopped momentarily and abruptly for a second in the middle of picking up the coffee tray. There came a brief flash from his eyes and a 'ping', then he picked up the tray, walked over with the coffee, set a cup in front of each of them and returned to his preparation plug. Katy picked up hers and sipped the hot drink as she listened.

"You see, last year Bob's brother, Mark, went to Gene Control for a minor adjustment, and he still hasn't come out. The family demanded to know what had happened to him and Bob went on the Shuttle to see if he could help, but when he got there they told him his brother had died and the funeral had been held the week before—they even showed him the burial casket."

"Well. I suppose even Gene Control make mistakes sometime." said Katy.

"The trouble was the dates didn't match. Bob had spoken to his brother on the day after he was supposed to have died. It was obvious all of the family believed implicitly in what Gene Control were saying and Mark's wife and children were grief stricken, but Bob felt very uneasy about it. He pretended to accept what they said without question then caught the next Shuttle home. Ever since then (what with that and Fergus wanting to grow up!) we've been making secret plans to leave." Katy was having difficulty taking it in, "I don't know anything about Outside—except that Ian's Mum went there after his Dad died. It's not possible to keep in contact with Outside, so we don't know if she's alive or dead. It must be very primitive there."

"I don't care. I can't live with this controlling atmosphere much longer. It would be a relief to live life as it used to be. After all, they had hospitals, nurses and doctors; houses; central heating; television; work and computers. It was just that they only lived for a short while—hardly anyone lived for more than a hundred years! Anyway—" Janice hesitated, then—"—Fergus has heard from Outside."

"You're joking!"

"No. The Children's Group for Grower's (they call themselves the 'ChiGGers' after a parasite you used to get from going barefoot Outside. Katy thought, 'all the more reason for not going there!') They are the ones who organise all the marches we've been seeing all year) have contacts who can get us out, so as soon as we can we're going." Katy's heart was pumping with apprehension, "Do Pogie and Michael know about this?"

"Pogie does, but you've kept Michael away from the last two rallies (when the Outsiders contacted them) and I told Pogie and Fergie they weren't to say anything about it unless we knew you and Ian were going Outside too."

"Thank you for that," said Katy feelingly," things have been very difficult lately, In fact we had decided to let Michael go to Gene Control at the same time as Fergie and Pogie. He'll be devastated when he knows that you're going."

"Please don't tell him until we're gone—if Gene Control find out God knows what will happen!"

"I can't believe Gene Control would do anything drastic—". Katy's voice tailed off uncertainly.

"You haven't experienced what we have, so I can't expect you to understand. We would like you and Ian and the children to come with us." Her eyes searched Katy's face, "It's all set up if you decide to come. Think about it. I must go home now, before anyone notices I'm changing my routine."

Katy saw Janice out of the door, then walked slowly to the garden room and absentmindedly began to spray the peach tree with multipurpose 'Fungisect', it was the only way it would survive indoors. Her mind began to leap from one thing to another *'I suppose it would still have to be sprayed Outside too. I wonder what it would be like? I can't believe Gene Control got rid of Bob's brother.'* "No! Ian would know if anything like that were happening!" she said aloud feeling comforted at this thought and continued with her tasks until Ian came home. Katy heard nothing from Janice for some days and the boys continued to go to the den in their free time as usual. Perhaps everything had been resolved, perhaps life would continue in the old familiar pattern.

PART FOUR

The internal Safe-screen buzzed—"Call for Control Affairs; Call for Control Affairs;—" Jim reluctantly activated the screen. The Head of Affairs' face beamed at him, "Good morning Jim!" Jim groaned inwardly *'What does he want now?'*

"Good morning Jack!" He forced a smile.

"How do you fancy a bit of good old-fashioned hunting Jim?"

"Sounds interesting. Where do we go for that?" He had learnt quite a few new dodges since being picked for 'THE TEAM', as the Head of Affairs called his government, but hunting was not amongst them.

"Outside!" said Jack nonchalantly. Jim sat up as though someone had let off a firework under his seat.

"Did you say—'Outside'?" he said unbelievingly.

"You heard me,—get your gear together and come to my office. I'll provide the guns and ammunition. We shall also need a few body-guards—I'll see to that too. Don't be afraid," he sneered, "we'll be back by lunch-time."

Jim de-activated the screen and sat back in his chair, *'I don't want to do do this"*. He thought, *'If I don't, I'll be out of favour. Out of favour out—of a job. It's got to be done!'* He sighed ruefully, *'Oh well, here goes'*.

CHAPTER 4

Ian came in so swiftly that the eating area door opened before the front door had shut, creating a sudden draught that blew peach blossom off the sprays Katy had brought into the kitchen to make the permanently dust free whiteness of the table look pretty. Katy jumped as he took her in his arms and the petals jumped too, and floated gently to the floor, rejected by the antigrav pristine table which would only allow specially treated objects to rest on it (the children had enormous fun trying to rest their elbows on it—Michael had once glued pieces of his Mother's neutralising work-mat to his sleeves and fooled Katy into thinking the table had gone wrong! It had been very difficult to get a replacement mat and Michael was banned from the games room for a week.)

"Have you seen Fergus's parents recently, Katy?"

"Not since Janice came round for coffee last week. Why?"

Once more her heart was speeding up with apprehension. "It's just that some strange things have been happening this week—you know Jaimie and Tom were brought into the Centre—well I asked after Tom, and got a very peculiar response. Jake Scott is a good friend of mine, and he happened to answer the Screen call I made. When I asked him how Tom was he looked all round to make sure no-one had heard, then said, "Trust me Ian! Ask NO questions about that family if you value your safety. Promise me!" I promised. "What do you think about that?"

Katy responded by telling him about her conversation with Jaimie, "I haven't heard from her since." Ian looked worried,

"As I left work just now, I saw Bob and Janice in reception. (The kids aren't here yet are they?)" he looked around.

"No. They'll be a few minutes yet." As Katy spoke the doors were activated almost as swiftly as when Ian came home, and she absently eyed the vacuum slot, activating it to suck up the fallen peach blossom. The blossom flew into the air with the draft from the door, followed inexorably by the nozzle, which slurped the petals in mid-air and slid noise-lessly back into the wall.

"Mum! Dad! Guess what? Fergie was picked up at Education Gate by the Centre Police this morning—we didn't get chance to talk to him." Michael was breathless and agitated. Ian frowned. "Did he seem surprised?"

"Yes. But they took him a little way from us and talked to him, then he shouted,

"Got to go—tell you later!" and they put him in a Medicopter and took him away."

Michael looked anxious.

"Don't worry about it—I'm sure there's a simple explanation." Ian caught Katy's eye momentarily and swiftly looked away for fear of betraying their worries. He put an arm around Michael's shoulders, "Did you tell the Master?

"Yes. he said it was "quite legitimate" and he had been informed all about it by Centre."

"Well, not to worry then."

Katy went to the door and looked into the hall, "Where are the others?"

Michael, his fears now more or less at rest, started to walk out of the room, "They've gone to the games area to start a game of Light Battles," he stopped, "Is it o.k. if I go and join in?"

"Off you go.—Welcome home, by the way," she smiled, giving him a quick kiss on the cheek. Michael laughed, "Hi, Mum".

Back in the eating area Ian and Katy sat at the table. Buttle was galvanised into activity, unplugging himself and zooming to the table. "Food not prepared. Time set 1.00p.m for family snack. Extra food required?" Katy pressed his 'Nil' Button for 'no change in plans' and he returned to his plug. Ian put his hand on Katy's, "All these things together add up to a very strange situation." he said.

"Yes. Our safe, secure existence suddenly seems to be turning into a nightmare." Katy was very apprehensive.

"Try not to worry just yet. I'm in a good position to find out about anyone at the Centre without being noticed—after all, it's my job to make sure the computers are working, and in that capacity I can run a brief safety check on all the surveillance screens—including the ones monitoring patients and prisoners. It would only be a snatch of information but it would be enough to gauge whether our friends are in trouble of any kind. Bearing in mind what Janice told you, the evidence seems to point to big problems. There are also little things I have been noticing over the years which by themselves are nothing, but as part of the present overall picture become a lot more serious."

"Perhaps Janice was right. Perhaps we should join them and go Outside."

"It may not come to that—come here and have a cuddle". Katy smiled—she always felt safe in Ian's arms.

The next day when Katy was programming Buttle after the others had left the house, the buzzer went. Katy pressed the mini-screen to see a man in a blue overall looking at her.

"—'morning Madam. Adam from Robofix at your service—here's my I.D."

He pressed it against the screen so that she could read it. Photo—definitely him—thought Katy.

Adam
from
ROBOFIX
'Faults Fixed Fast'

'—*funny, I know there are minor faults with Buttle, but we hadn't reported them.*' Katy thought. "That seems to be in order, but I haven't reported any faults".

"I know Madam. But as we have been receiving a great many complaints about minor faults in programming it's Company Policy to put things right so that customers suffer no inconvenience. Your model is obsolete now, so we want to check it out and make sure you get the ninety-nine year value we guaranteed. May I come in?"

"Well, that's what I call service!" said Katy, letting Adam in. He mentioned all the minor problems Katy had been experiencing, and removed Buttle's top garments (he was dressed to resemble a Victorian butler) and the control panel on his chest, adjusting a few micro-toms and replacing two. "You shouldn't have any more trouble, Madam—at least, not from the robot." He looked at her meaningfully.

"I don't know what you mean." Katy backed away from Adam uneasily.

"I believe you have been experiencing unusual happenings recently—friends talking about Outside, and people disappearing—children joining the 'ChiGGers'."

"H—no-one I know personally has disappeared." Katy had been going to ask how he knew—'that was close—I nearly gave myself away!'

"Don't be afraid, I'm just letting you know that you have more friends than you know—we are watching, and when you need help we will be in touch." Then, as though he had said nothing out of the ordinary, "Always at your service—'faults fixed fast'—here's my card—call this number if you have any more trouble with the Robot—or any other problems," he looked at her meaningfully, "Good morning."

"Good morning." Katy let him out and watched his blue helivan, with the ROBOFIX logo on the sides, take off and soar almost silently into the sky.

PART FIVE

They were in a jungle. Not the well-tamed 'jungle' of the Gene Control area but an unbelievably thorny, squelchy, hot and steamy place. Jim felt as though eyes were watching him from amongst the trees—and he was right. This was Outside, and everything was truly wild and definitely not under control! He tried not to feel worried, but the bodyguards seemed a lot further away than he would have liked. Something touched his shoulder and with a yell he swung round and fired a shot—at a liana hanging down from the trees.

"What are you doing, Jim?" Jack sounded angry and impatient, "I told you! Wait until the bodyguards flush out our prey!"

"Sorry Jack."

There was a sudden thud, and a noisy rustling as something rushed away through the undergrowth. Jack lifted his gun and fired. There was a loud scream, then the rustling began again. "There he goes Jim! Shoot him!"

They had reached a clearing made by a fallen tree, and in front of them something crouched on the opposite side of the clearing. Jim raised his gun and looked through the sight magnifier, his finger tightened on the trigger, then he realised that the eye he could see through the sight was human. He lowered his gun and turned to Jack,

"That's a human being, Jack!" Jack tutted impatiently and fired just as their 'prey' took off through the trees and disappeared from view.

The Head lowered his gun and looked at Jack with scorn, "Why on earth didn't you shoot whilst you had the chance? We'll probably go back with no score now!"

'—*no score? Does he really expect me to shoot people for fun?*' Privately—Jack was horrified, publicly (with fears of losing his lucrative Government post) he meekly said, "You didn't say we were hunting people."

"People? These aren't 'people'—they're human detritus. Imperfect failures from Gene Control. As you can see," he continued sneeringly, "—they are not capable of development, can only live as animals—and animals are what they have become. Therefore they are lawful prey."

"I see where you are coming from, but it's going to be a while before I can get my head around this." *'like never'* he thought. "I've never been hunting before in my life, so you can understand my surprise, Head." *'and that's putting it mildly'.*

"Ah! I didn't realise. That explains it. Must admit, the first time I went shooting it took me a couple of hours to hype myself up to kill an animal—but once I mastered it I was hooked. Never mind Jim—there's always next time !"

"Mmm." Jim was non-committal, but thought, *'over my dead body'.* They returned to the shuttle and went back Inside.

CHAPTER 5

In the Computer room Ian was ostensibly checking the security cameras—in reality he was looking for any trace of his friends and their children. Ward after ward, room after room he scanned (doing the deep search for off-camera areas). He was taking a big risk here, for this search was only due to be carried out on a quarterly basis and there was still a month to run before it was due. The door slid open and Jake Scott shot into Security Viewing like a rocket and stopped, panting, under the security camera. "You're looking for your friends again." He stated. "I've told you that is very dangerous. I know where they are—contact me on Security Wave after work."

Ian couldn't wait to get home and contact Jake, he hurried into the house and greeted Katy with a kiss, "Come with me and listen to this." He led her to the Call Screen and punched in Jake's call number. Jake's face appeared fuzzily on-screen, almost obliterated by the security codes.

"Your friends are in Deep Security with their children (except Pogie and Pam Moore). We are in touch with a rescue service—do not—repeat—DO NOT attempt to find them. Wait for our contact to call." The Screen went blank. Ian and Katy looked at each other.

"I'm very frightened," said Katy, "some funny things have been going on lately."

"I know." Ian hugged her as they snuggled down into the viewing seat.

"A technician from Robofix called this morning." Katy was looking down at her fingers. Ian was surprised, "Had you reported any faults?"

"No! He said it was an automatic call in answer to several minor complaints from other customers, to ensure satisfactory service and long term product viability." She hesitated. "Go on." Ian was interested.

"He said not to worry about friends' disappearances, that we had more friends than we knew and that they would be in touch when it became necessary."

"That's more or less what Jake said. So I suppose we'd better keep to our routine as though nothing was wrong."

"Perhaps we had,—hungry?" Katy turned to look at him, "I've programmed Buttle to make us a snack."

*   *   *

The family fell into a routine—children went to school, came home, had a snack, went to the woods or played at home. Ian went to work and Katy did the home tasks, she also signed on at Education for 'Cre-art' Classes as she usually did at this time of year, this time choosing to do painting once more. Apart from Pogie and Pam asking a lot of questions about their parents, which Katy was finding even harder to answer as the days went by, there were few difficulties. She pointed out to the children that too many questions to Gene Control might result in Pogie and Pam being sent to Child Rescue, which they didn't fancy at all. "I'm sure when Mummy is well enough to come home, Control will get in touch with us," Katy said, hugging them, "Try to be patient and if no-one has contacted us in two weeks time, Ian will make enquiries."

*   *   *

Katy waited until the children had left for school, and over breakfast talked to Ian, "It's three weeks since Pogie and Pam came and we've heard nothing," she sounded uneasy. Ian shrugged, "Well, we can't do anything until we hear who is helping us and what they're going to do." He finished his fruit juice and slid along the curved smoothness of the seat to her. Kate took his hand, "Can't you talk to Jake again?"

"Better not—he sounded very worried, "—he did say wait until we hear. I must go, or I'll be late." They hugged each other, then pulled back and gazed into each other's eyes. Katy touched his nose, "Love you." her voice was soft and throaty with emotion and physical feeling.

"Wish I could stay." Ian pressed his lips to hers and for a moment they both felt that tangible merging of auras which usually ended in passionate loving, Ian groaned, then tore himself away with a ruefully blown kiss as he paused momentarily in the doorway.

Katy sighed, and went into the eating area to programme Buttle, for some reason this proved impossible, whatever she did no programme could be set up, so she called Robo-fix. A young, attractive, girlish face smiled at her from the screen.

"Robo-fix. Faults fixed fast! Mrs. Stone, Robofix are aware of the faults you have experienced this morning—Adam is on his way, Buttle will be fixed today! Thank you for calling."

'*—there must be an electronic link from Buttle to the robot manufacturers.*' Katy thought, remembering how Adam had come to fix Buttle without being notified. The Viewing Screen bleeped, and Adam's face appeared, "Robofix calling!" He smiled into the viewer. Katy said, "Come in Adam." and eyed the door opener (these had been programmed for family only). Adam carried a large, wrapped, humanoid shape in through the door.

"Good morning! This is your replacement robot—we have to take the old model away as it has broken down during the guarantee period. The new model is more up-to-date." Katy was surprised,

"We haven't had Buttle all that long—are you sure he needs replacing? We've grown quite attached to him." Adam smiled, "You'll get even more attached to this one, Mrs. Stone! Our robots are so realistic now you'll think he is human—did you notice the girl on the Call Screen this morning? (I was informed of your call)".

"Yes, I did. I thought what an attractive girl she was."

"One of last year's models."

"You mean she's a **robot**?"

"Certainly. You wouldn't have known if I hadn't told you—would you?" He unwrapped the new robot, which looked so real Katy felt a cold shiver down her spine. "It's voice activated, has the power of speech and is capable of operating all the working devices in the modern home—vacuum wall system; cleaning booth (it is able to go into the booth for self cleaning) saving its owners a great deal of time. It can also check finances and order appropriate food according to family preferences!"

"I don't think we can afford this. We had to think twice before we ordered Buttle."

"There will be no extra charge, as I said, your original robot has developed faults which we know are just the beginning of major problems. I shall take it away, and will be calling to give you advice on use of the replacement—it is quite a sophisticated model. Before I go I will show you the basics of programming for meals and cleaning the house—on no account must you try anything other than what I teach you today. This model will not be replaced if it develops faults due to your own mistakes." They spent all morning on the tutorial and by the time it was over Katy's head was spinning with instructions. She thankfully waved goodbye to Adam and went back into the house.

"Good afternoon, Madam. Is there anything you require?" The new robot smiled and inclined his head politely as he spoke (there was no way Katy could refer to him as 'it'). The brass buttons on his uniform gleamed expensively and you could have cut yourself on the old-fashioned (permanent) creases in his trousers. His whole demeanor was redolent of Victorian servitude and propriety—and Katy found him rather intimidating. "No thank you, James," (that was the name she had chosen for him—solid and old-fashioned as was everything about him), "Your programming is finished for today." James retreated to the re-charging point where Buttle used to stand and attempted to become part of the furnishings.

When Ian came home from the Centre, he was amazed by James, "Strange they should give us an expensive replacement when Buttle's faults were so minor. We'll have to be careful with him—I'm glad they're giving you tuition—how much is that costing?"

"It's all in with the package—let's just enjoy it while we can, I feel as though they might take him back at any moment!"

The children arrived. "Where's Buttle—and where did he come from ?" Michael looked James up and down in awe.

"Don't touch anything!" Ian warned, "James is his name, and he's a very superior replacement. Your mother is having tuition and no-one else is to meddle—we could have serious problems with an out of control, incorrectly programmed robot!" Michael backed away respectfully, and so did the other children. Pogie and Pam chorused, "We won't touch James, Ian."

"I won't even go near him," shuddered Sarah, "—he's creepy!"

"Hello, Sarah!" James smiled at her, "You don't need to be afraid of me, I'm only here to help."

"Aa-ah!" Sarah screamed, "How did he know my name?"

"I have been programmed to know the names of everyone living in this house." James gestured at all the children, "Pogie and Pam—how are you today?—and Michael, I hope you are going to do your homework today! I hope you will all enjoy the snacks I have prepared for your lunch—it is ready for consumption at your convenience." He began to prepare the table and laid out a different snack for everyone's preference—salmon and salad for the adults, toast and assorted preserves for Pogie and Pam, fruit and buttered toast for Sarah and sardine sandwiches for Michael.

"I think I can learn to like you, James," said Michael with his mouth full, glancing appreciatively at the hot chocolate drink which was his favourite.

"Thank you Michael, the feeling is mutual." Michael nudged his father,

"I thought robots had no feelings." he whispered. Ian frowned and shook his head, James was so realistic, he instinctively found himself protecting the robot's supposedly non-existent feelings. After their snack, the children all went off to the woods to improve their den. The boys had decided that they were going to build an annexe for the girls—it was getting a bit crowded in the den now they were bigger, and if the boys were allowed to progress to puberty they would need even more space (always supposing they still wanted to use the den).

Ian and Katy went into the viewing room and watched an old 'Smeely' (a combination of 'smelly and 'feely') which had first been developed when they were in their teens, they sat holding hands as they used to do when they first met, full of nostalgia. "When it's over, shall we go for a walk in the woods like we used to?" Ian whispered in Katy's ear. She nodded, eyes glued to the screen as the hero handed a bouquet of roses to his lover and the room was filled with the fragrance of the flowers. Finally, as Katy wiped away her tears, generated by the happy ending, Ian pulled her to her feet and kissed her, "Come with me to the woods!" And they went laughing down the road as though all the years between now and then had never happened and they were teenagers again.

At the den, the boys had decided how they were going to build the extension, but as they had forgotten to bring tools, Michael decided to go home and fetch his school pack, "There will be enough tools for everyone to do something in there."

"I hope Fergus won't mind us changing things—I wish he was here." Pogie said wistfully.

"I'm sure he won't mind," Michael said on his way out of the den, "I won't be long."

Back in the house, Michael went into the Antigrav lift to the first floor—he had always enjoyed the lovely feeling it gave him to be free of the force—and picked up his pack of tools before anti-gravving down. As he came quietly out of the lift into the viewing room there were two strange men going through Ian's film collection—he stopped, undecided what to do and wondering how they had manage to get in. Their backs were turned to him. One said, "There's a lot of suspect stuff here—shows too much involvement with the past." the other agreed. "I think there's a danger to the Centre here."

"Yes. And that combined with his involvement with the other suspects makes it certain we'll have to take the whole family—" he turned and saw Michael staring at them, "Quick! Don't let him get away!" The two men grabbed him, "Leave me alone!" Michael shouted. One of the men grabbed a cloth from his pocket and stuffed it into Michael's mouth.

"Blindfold him—shut your eyes boy!" The man twisted Michael's arms behind his back whilst plastitape was smoothed across his eyes, the gag was plastitaped into his mouth and his legs were taped together. Suddenly Michael found himself released, and losing his balance fell to the floor in front of the seating, his face uncomfortably buried in the carpet. He managed to turn his face to the side, but could not see what was happening. "Look out!" shouted one of the men. Michael heard a dull, smacking thud, "Uuuuph!" grunted the other man. With a loud scream, something large flew through the air and landed with a crash against something hard, there was the sound of running feet padding across the floor, then another, cut-off scream and a couple of sharp, smacking sounds followed by a sighing groan and a slithering thump. Michael could not understand what was happening. He heard foot-steps, the doors slid open and closed again, and after a few minutes the doors opened again and strange voices were talking, "Good job we left a guard here-"

"Sh-shsh! The boy's not deaf! Let's get this mess cleared up before the family come home."

There were sounds of sweeping, and dragging. The doors opened and shut, then after a while they opened again and someone knelt at Michael's side. A man's voice whispered,

"Don't be afraid Michael, we're friends of your parents. You can tell them what happened—but not the other children, you must keep it between you and the adults. I'm going to remove the gag and untape your legs, but keep the plaster over your eyes for a few minutes until you're sure we've gone. Tell your parents not to mention this to anyone else. We'll meet again later. Goodbye for now." Michael heard him leave, then began to remove the tape from his eyes—fortunately it had almost missed his eyebrows—although it did take a few hairs with it.

"Ouch!" Michael removed the last of the plaster and looked around the room—there wasn't a sign that anything had happened. With a puzzled frown he took it into the eating area and put it in the waste disposal. James stood in Buttle's old place, "Good afternoon, Michael. The evening meal is being prepared, make sure you are not late—you don't want it to end up in the waste—disposal, I'm sure!"

"I won't be late, thank you James!" He wandered into the viewing room once more. Two men had cleared up—there must have been a mess of some kind—but who was it who had rescued him from his attackers? It must have been someone else who had hidden in the house before he came in—it was very puzzling, but he had things to do—the others were waiting for him! He set off with his tools resolving to keep the strange happenings to himself until he saw his parents.

*   *   *

After the others had gone to bed, Michael antigravved down to tell his parents what had happened. It was a relief to unburden himself as he had been bursting to tell someone. Ian and Katy listened to him with growing concern. Ian distractedly pushed back his hair. "It seems our worries were well-founded. Well, Michael, you wanted to be grown-up—now you're getting a taste of adulthood! We must keep this to ourselves and not worry the other three. The less people who are watching out for trouble the better."

"Where were they were going to 'take the family'?" wondered Katy, "And I wonder who it was that fought off your attackers, Michael?" Michael shrugged,

"I haven't the faintest idea Mum!" Ian was pacing up and down the viewing room searching the soft resilience of the plastiflooring, something glinted near Katy's foot where she sat on the viewing seat—he picked it up. "A brass button!" He held his hand out, palm down for their inspection." Katy took it from him, "I think I—", as she spoke Katy rose and walked across the room and through the door. They followed to find Katy in the eating area holding the button against those on James' pristine jacket. "It matches!"

Michael looked into the robot's eyes, "Can I help you, Michael?" James inclined his head politely. "I think you already have," said Michael, "—one of your buttons came off in the viewing room."

"As I said earlier, I am only here to help." James said calmly, taking the button and re-placing it skilfully—it seemed to glide into place and looked as though it had never moved.

"Was it you who fought off those men?" Michael looked into James' eyes, but the robot's eyes were blank. "I don't know what you mean, Michael," he said.

PART SIX

The call screen was screaming at maximum volume as Jim arrived at his office, "Call for Minister of Subject Control; Call for Minister of Subject Control! Call for Minister of Subject Control! . . . . "

'—*not even allowed to get in through the door! Hope to God Jack doesn't expect me to go hunting Outside again!*' The door shutting smoothly behind him, Jim hurled his coat to the robot (latest model, too realistic for comfort. Jim had expressed his fears to the Head but they had been dismissed as needless worries) who (no, which) caught it deftly—and activated the Call Screen, not from any desire to speak to the Head, but to get rid of the nagging voice.

"At last, Minister! We haven't time for late arrivals in this building—we have pressing problems." Stung by the injustice, Jim tried to defend himself. "I am actually ten minutes earl—".

"For goodness sake, will you stop wasting time, Minister."

'*Oops! No point trying to call him 'Jack' today.*' "What is the problem, Head Minister?"

"That's more like it! There have been several security problems in the South of the Control Area. We have had to place two families in Deep Security—and yesterday morning we lost two Security Officers."

"You mean they're dead?" Death was a dirty word in Gene Control.

"No!" The Head sounded impatient. "They were sent to investigate at the home of one of our Internal Security Team from the Centre, Ian Stone, and no-one has seen them since! This is your responsibility. Why is it I know all about it and you know nothing? Don't forget what I said about your job, Minister—there is a line and it's on it!"

"That was if we had any more marches from the Chiggers—".

"Any shortcomings will have the same effect. Find out what is happening—we don't want to lose any more Eternals to Outside. If we do, we'll both be out of a job! I expect to hear your updates hourly—leave messages if I'm not in the office."

"Very well, Sir." The call screen went blank. Jim shivered. '*Why didn't I hear about this? Somebody's trying to make things difficult for me—probably got an eye on my job!* He began to investigate, beginning with a Screencall to Gene Control about Ian Stone and family. As soon as he activated the screen, inside his updated robot a latent communication system was triggered and coded messages sent Outside. Jim addressed the agent on screen, "What are your findings regarding the Stone family? Did you place a bugging device?" "Yes sir".

"Let me have a copy of the recording chip." The agent in security looked worried. "I can't do that, sir, because the bug hasn't been triggered yet".

"Why not? Why wasn't it done on the spot?"

"The agents forgot."

"Well, for goodness sake use distance activation—you know how to do it, don't you? If not you will be replaced by someone who does!" Inside his updated robot the communication system was again triggered and coded messages sent Outside.

CHAPTER 6

The early morning rain was falling as Katy looked out of the window.

'God's in his Heaven and all's well with the artificial eco-system!' she thought wryly to herself. Poetry had always been a particular joy of hers, but much of the old poetry about natural phenomena had been rendered spurious by way of the technical progress of the Control Centre. Rain was programmed to fall at the least inconvenient time for society in general, between six and eight in the morning or eleven o'clock to one o'clock at night on alternate days according to necessity. This was all very convenient, but Katy sometimes yearned to experience the variety of weather she read about in books—thunderstorms or gales (but perhaps not tornadoes or floods!) Katy shivered and moved quickly away from the window. Already cleansed and dressed, she made sure the children were getting ready and anti-gravved down to make sure James's programmer had worked. (Buttle's later vagaries had left her feeling a little insecure and she didn't want to find breakfast had gone into the waste-disposal because the timer was faulty.) Breakfast was ready, bacon (pre-formed), eggs, as they always were and assorted fruit. James had set the table and was laying out the meal in transparent heat-sealers and dishes ready for attack. The children rushed in hungrily and began to demolish the meal—Katy and Ian usually waited until they had left for school, it made for a peaceful breakfast and serious talks where necessary. As soon as they had said goodbye to the children, Ian and Katy settled down to their meal. "Thank Goodness for robots!" Ian said as he relished the crisp bacon, and eggs done to perfection, "You wouldn't get this Outside!" The viewing screen bleeped, it was Adam from Robo-fix. "Good morning Mr. Stone—I'm very glad to meet you." Ian, slightly bemused, shook Adam's offered hand.

"I'm here for your wife's second lesson in robot operation. Katy laughed nervously. "Well, Adam. The first lesson was quite easy—I hope the second is similar." Adam smiled and looked at Ian,

—

"Perhaps you would like to sample the first part of the tuition—if you have a little time?" Ian checked the time, "Yes. I'd like that. I do have a few minutes". Adam put a finger to his lips and beckoned to them to follow him, talking as he went into the Viewing Room and showed them a mini-chip which he placed under the Viewing Screen. "Mrs. Moore, if you'd like to fetch your new robot into the viewing room, we can work in comfort." Katy called James with her remote. He walked confidently into the room, and once more Ian wondered at his apparent humanity, "You called, Madam?"

Adam put a finger to his lips and said, "I am going to give you the lesson now, and will record this one for you as it is more difficult." Next Adam produced a remote control device and pointed it towards the screen, then motioned them towards the kitchen.

"I'm sorry about the cloak and dagger bit, but there must be no suspicion of Robofix. Briefly—our agents discovered a bug under your screen which now has a pre-recorded lesson playing next to it whilst I give you important information. We are going to provide you with robots in the form of each of your family, including Pogie and Pam. They have been programmed to behave as a family at home. At the right moment we shall spirit you away to Outside where you will be completely safe. We shall also be rescuing Mr. and Mrs. Mailer and Mr. and Mrs. Briden and Fergus. This will all happen on Saturday when your heads of government are relaxing and off guard. There will be three more lessons during which we shall leave instructions for you. The bug has to be left functioning, otherwise Gene Control will be suspicious. All you have to do is behave normally. Let the children know you have a special treat for them on Saturday and tell them it will mean staying out very late. No questions now, we must get back to the lesson!"

They moved quietly back into the viewing room where the lesson was still playing, Adam's voice offered a few more instructions, and said, "Have you understood that?"

Adam signalled to Katy, "Well." she said, "It is rather a lot to take in all at once, but with the recording you have made I think we shall manage very well!"

Ian agreed, "Thank you very much, Adam, that was very interesting—I am very impressed with your robot. I'm sure between us we shall not make any mistakes." Adam smiled, "It's very important that you don't attempt to deal with anything other than what I have taught you today as you could damage the robot." He turned to Katy, "I must congratulate you on the way you have handled James so far, and I'm sure you will manage well. Here is your recording, I hope you find it useful." He removed the mini-chip from under the screen, placed it in a protective package and handed it to Katy. Ian checked the time again,

"I shall have to leave, otherwise I'm going to be late." He kissed Katy who watched him walk down the path with Adam, talking together. After they had gone Katy was in shock. She turned on the viewing screen, not to watch, but to give the bug something to listen to whilst she gathered the thoughts which fought for attention in her mind. OUTSIDE! What would it be like? How would the look-alike robots manage to hide the family's absence from the house? Would they all be safe? How could she behave normally? How could she wait until Saturday? Who had placed the bug? She felt afraid that she would miss everything about Gene Control and wondered what it would be like to die—

PART SEVEN

Jim cursed as he heard his call screen screaming again through the locked door. He checked the time, "I'm early, so what's the trouble?" he cursed under his breath as he eye-balled the keypad and squeezed in before the door had finished opening. He flung his coat at the robot as usual and hurried over to the screen which activated as he sat down. "Ah! Jim! Early bird Eh?" The Head Minister smiled at him from the screen. "I would like you to come with me on Saturday-I'm going to give you another opportunity to score Outside."

'What am I going to say now? I don't want to kill anyone—or anything.'

"Well, thank you Head." *'softly, softly—'* "It's very kind of you to take the trouble, but I have to keep track of those security problems you mentioned the other day. I had a bug placed in the Stones' house, which is being monitored round the clock. Everything seems to be in order at the moment, but I need to investigate the relationships between the Stones and those two families in Deep Security." The Head Minister frowned.

"I'm very disappointed in you, Minister. If—." Jim thought it politic to interrupt before any threats were made.

"I am extremely disappointed too, Head Minister. I have greatly enjoyed our excursions, and was looking forward to this one, but I cannot risk missing anything at this stage—I believe there is a danger of Eternals going Outside—there have been rumours!" The Head seemed mollified,

"Ah! I see your problem. Well, perhaps the following weekend?" Jim breathed a sigh of relief, *'-saved by the skin of my teeth!'* Aloud he said,

"Thank you for your understanding, Head. I look forward to our next excursion!" *'how shall I get out of that when it comes around?'* He shrugged resignedly as the screen was de-activated.

CHAPTER 7

Katy (feeling a little paranoid) thought she had better listen to the second lesson in case she had to answer questions about it. To her relief it was mostly revision of the first lesson she had had with only a few new points to learn. Adam had cleverly given instructions as though she was present in the room, '—now, if you would demonstrate how you would programme the robot to prepare a meal Mrs. Stone—.' (sounds of bleeps and buttons being pressed)

"Excellent, you have remembered that very well,—now, cancel that programme. Wonderful—you are a quick learner! Now I'd like you to demonstrate programming for house cleansing and cancel that". Katy did as he asked. "Well done! I don't think we need any revision of those instructions. I will now instruct you in some simple maintenance procedures."

Katy followed the new instructions, which were also shown on the viewing screen, with an enlarged programming pad. There didn't seem to be anything mind-challenging in the instructions, she supposed the rest of the lessons were just going to be a cover for Adam's supportive visits and instructions about their escape. A shiver went up her spine and she turned off the recording, replacing the mini-chip in its container. Most of the information they received from Gene Control about Outside emphasised the backwardness and lack of amenities, the antediluvian hospitals and most of all, early death. How many years would she and Ian have left together? She closed her mind to her terrifying thoughts and went to do some Creatart for her next class, forgetting as she became absorbed in her three-dimensional project that for her there would be no more classes.

The days passed quickly, Ian managed to warn Michael about the bug so that he remembered only to talk to them about his experiences whilst they were on the top floor or outside the house. Adam came for the 'lessons'—sometimes it seemed to Katy that he was part of the family and life seemed so normal it seemed things would go on for ever just as they were. In the moments when she remembered they were going Outside it felt as though her heart and stomach were somersaulting over each other and she felt half full of dread—half full of excitement. Adam told them they were to take very few belongings, only a few valuables—enough to fit in their picnic containers—their valuable transporter, all the furnishings, tools, toys, films, games and clothes—even James—would have to be left behind. "Don't worry—there is a home waiting for you Outside—we guarantee all escapees that they will be just as well off there as inside Gene Control! There is work, entertainment (the best entertainment being the whole out-door world) and what is more your older children, Jack and Simon are also Outside with their families!" Katy and Ian stared, amazed. "After all these years?"

"Yes. They came outside without help quite recently. It was very difficult for them—but you will hear about all that from them." Katy's eyes filled with tears, "No wonder we haven't heard from them—Oh Ian!" Her head rested against his shoulder as Ian put his arm around her. So there would be compensations for going Outside, even if technology was a little backward, she thought.

Saturday came all too soon and everyone was up at the crack of dawn The children were delighted to be going on a picnic—Pam and Pogie had never been to the beach and were beside themselves with excitement, trying to help get things ready and getting under every-one's feet. Finally, exasperated with trying to remember all of Adam's instructions, prepare the food and treading on one or the other children, Katy said, "Pogie and Pam!"

"Yes, Katy?"

"You are not used to getting ready for picnics—why don't you just find a few of the things you might like to do on the journey? Bring your favourite clothes for going out too—we might go to the new restaurant for an evening meal."

"Shall we get ours as well?" chorused Sarah and Michael. Kate nodded, and the four rushed to the anti-grav and disappeared for a while.

"Phew! I thought we'd never be ready—let's get finished before they come down again!" Ian wrapped sandwiches as fast as Buttle made them, Katy sorted out the fruit, drinks and beach seats and she and Ian ferried them out to the transporter. At last everything was ready—children and necessaries in their places. Katy and Ian took a last look round. In the kitchen Katy whispered brokenly, "We shan't spend another hundred years here—I've loved living here with you." Ian took her hand and squeezed it. "Don't look back my Love, or the children will see you crying and they'll know something's up. Come on."

They smiled at each other, Katy seeing Ian through a circle of rainbows as the sun gleamed on her tears. She wiped them away with her fingers and they left the house to climb into the transporter.

*   *   *

In the event the only things needed to occupy everyone were two packs of cards as they had a Bridge marathon lasting almost the length of the journey, as Pogie and Pam were just as addicted to the game as Michael and Sarah (parents versus the children in pairs) Much whispering from Pam to Sarah—'Ian must have the King of Hearts, he responded No Trumps pspsp.' Parents winning for once '—too many cooks.' Katy whispered. There was a familiar bleep from the dashboard, "Warning! Ten minutes to arrival. Please access the wheel." There was no delay this time—Ian was on tenterhooks—in no time the seats were adjusted and his hands were on the wheel. The children chattered excitedly in the back seat about the things they were going to do on the beach, oblivious to the adults growing apprehension. The wheels made contact with the road as the car adjusted itself to off-Auto-route travel and they rolled easily into the car-park at the beach. Katy breathed a sigh of relief to see there were no other vehicles. The children were out of the car before Ian had organised the gears and preset the locks. Katy called through the open door.

"What about your swimming things?" On the brink of going down the bank, the four halted abruptly and looked at each other. Michael said nobly, "You two go down and have a look round—Sarah and I will help with the picnic stuff." Sarah nodded approvingly.

"Yes—you can help reload when we go home." With screams and whoops of delight Pogie and Pam disappeared over the edge as the others walked back to their parents. Eager to join their friends, Michael and Sarah didn't notice there were far more bags than usual to take down to the beach. They struggled down the sandy bank on their bottoms dragging spades, shrimping nets, bags and towels—an ageless cameo of children down the ages rushing to the glorious freedom of the beach. Pogie and Pam came hurtling to meet them and in no time the four were in their costumes and cavorting and splashing in the waves, leaving a heap of belongings near the rocks (smooth and shiny from years of being leaned against) where Ian and Katy had been picnicking with their children for a lifetime. Ian and Katy saw them from the top of the bank as they stood laden with what were now their only worldly goods. Katy's eyes filled with tears again, "Oh! Why do I always have to **cry**?" she asked the sky through gritted teeth. Ian put down everything he was carrying and put his arm round her,

"Because you are a wonderful, caring woman, and I thank God you are mine! Go ahead and cry—the children are too busy and too far away to notice. I know why you are crying—this is the last time we shall visit the beach where you and I met, and where we have taken all our children—two of whom we have not seen for years and who will shortly be available to us again. We don't know how we shall be living in the future, but at least we have that to look forward to. Does that make you feel better?" Katy turned to him gratefully, "Yes! You always find the right thing to say—and you're right—it will be lovely to see Jack and Simon again."

"Who knows? You may be a Granny by now!"

Katy began to laugh, "If I'm a Granny then you're a Grandad!"

"If I didn't have so much to carry I'd get you for that!" Ian laughed as they struggled down the bank to the rocks. They passed the day happily with swimming, beach games and the picnic—then Ian and Katy dozed for a while in the shade of the rocks whilst Michael and Sarah showed their friends assorted wild-life in the rock-pools which they had so far only seen in the 'smeelies'. Pogie was amazed, "I didn't know all this was here!" He spread his arms as 'though he wanted to embrace the whole scene. "It's much better than the pool—more exciting!" "Yes!" called his twin as she raced down to the sea. "You never know when the next wave is coming!" Pam rushed into the waves, lifting her legs higher and higher as the water deepened. "AA-aah!" she screamed as an unexpectedly large wave broke over her head, and she came out the other side spluttering and gasping. Michael looked at the setting sun,

"It's nearly time to go home." He said, "I hope Gene Control never stop us from using the beach—hardly anyone else bothers with it these days."

"Is it 'Outside?" Pogie asked Michael wonderingly as he tried to pull a sea anemone from a rock without success. "No, of course not—that would make it too easy for people to leave!"

"It looks as though we could just walk out now—there's only that wood in the way!" Pogie sat on a rock and gestured towards the trees on the skyline.

"Yes, it does look like that, but the wood is not safe and there's a barrier to keep the wild animals out—you can't see it from here."

"Kids! Come and clear up now". They turned to see Ian waving. "O-oh! I don't want to leave yet!" Pogie sounded disappointed. Michael grabbed his hand, "Come on—I'll race you back! We'll play Light zapping again when we get home!" The boys hurtled along the beach, trying to catch the girls who were already racing back.

Silently the Helimoth settled on the beach with its deceptively fragile blades fluttering in circles as the sun sank in a glow of turquoise, gold and scarlet, the final slice of its burning globe floating above its reflection in the fiery sea. "Look!" whispered Sarah, tugging her father's sleeve, "What's that Dad?" Ian looked up from the packed beach equipment as he pulled the fastening tight. Katy gasped,

"I thought they weren't coming after all".

"Who's 'they'?' chorused Michael and the twins. The group stood transfixed as three figures came running up to them. "Mr. and Mrs. Stone? Peter Marsden with Outside Rehab," he shook hands with Ian and Katy, "I'm so sorry we're so late—we had a slight problem with Gene Control—we are being followed." The first of their rescuers stopped to get his breath.

"You must board the Moth now! Give me your keys Ian." Ian handed them over. "Michael? Sarah? Go with John—twins? With Malcolm—follow me QUICKLY!" They all rushed down the beach, under the Moth and were floated abruptly through an aperture there by the anti-grav. On board, pulled aboard by two men and with gravity unexpectedly re-established they regained their balance by falling into each other. Marsden and Malcolm steadied them, apologising profusely. Six figures rose from the HeliMoth's seats. Katy gasped, pointing, "Look! It's us!' Like a mirror image, Katy, Ian, Sarah and Pogie and his sister walked towards them. Peter Marston gave Ian's keys to his 'twin' and the whole imitation family was anti-gravved to the beach. Ushered into the vacated seats Ian and Katy saw 'themselves' trudging up the beach with some of the equipment they had brought with them that morning and watched with feelings of envy, apprehension for the future and grief-stricken nostalgia for the only life they had known. 'So sorry for the rush, people, we usually lift up only one or two at a time!" Shown to one of several rows of seats, still slightly breathless the children began to ask questions, "Mum—Dad—what's happening?" "Where are we going?" Michael and Sarah were bewildered. Ian and Katy edged into the row of seats opposite the children. Ian looked at Katy questioningly. Katy took his arm, "We must tell them—there's no going back now!' Ian leaned across Katy, "We're going Outside!" There was a stunned silence as the children looked from one to the other in amazement. Peter Marsden walked to the pilot, "You can take off now Frank—everyone's settled." He slipped into the seat behind the pilot as the HeliMoth took off rapidly, canting alarmingly to one side, 'So sorry for the rush, people, we usually lift up only one or two at a time!" From behind the Moth came the sound of laser-fire.

PART EIGHT

Computer Vision was off. Jim did not want to be disturbed. Thoughts buzzed around in his head arguing and fighting with each other like separate entities.

'The Money's good!' 'Is it really worth it?' 'You're living in luxury!' 'Yes, but how long can I go on living with myself?' 'I'm not going hunting again!' '—and what about Gene Control?' 'Don't want to think about that!' 'You have to!'

Jim tried to keep the images at bay but it was impossible. That poor deranged man—his mind destroyed by Gene Control's meddling—not to mention his battered, bloodied wife ('although at least she's going to recover'). And all the others! He tried to erase the images.

'I could end up there!' 'Yes! If you don't play along with Jack! After all, he's responsible for Gene Control.' The images replayed against his will, *'And all the others!' 'Don't think about it'*. He could still hear the screams in Deep Security. He had only been there once—that was enough for any normal person. Realisation dawned *'I can't live with it any longer!'* He had to get out or go insane! There was only one answer—Outside! As he tried to think of some way of getting out of Gene Control without being found out—and prevented from leaving, his eyes, unseeing, roved over the desk and accidentally re-activated Computer Vision. "Oh! there you are Jim—you must be very busy, I've been trying to get hold of you for some time!" Jim pulled himself together,

"Yes—I've been finishing investigations into contacts with the Stone family."

"What's the matter? You haven't found more problems?" Jack's voice rose higher with the stress.

"No, not at all sir. The bug is working and I have spoken to Bug Reception today—in fact if you want I can play you a recording of last night's activities at their home!" Jim heard a relieved sigh, "Not to worry Jim! I was just going to ask you if you're ready for today's outing." *'Blast! It's Saturday—I'd better play along—'* "Of course, Jack!" Jim's eyes took another trip, to the corner where his golf-clubs stood, "My clubs are ready—" Jack interrupted, "We're not playing golf—we're going shooting again and I hope your aim has improved. Just to make sure, I've got a state of the art weapon for you—wait 'til you see it—it is incredible! See you in my office—five minutes."

Jack's face disappeared from the screen. Miserably Jim took himself off to his boss's office where Jack lovingly caressed a wicked looking gun. "It's almost impossible to miss with this Jim. Point and press and it will find it's mark—I could blow a hole big enough to jump through in this wall! Just make sure you press the right button—red for people, black for buildings!" He aimed and sighted and for a moment Jim thought he was actually going to do it! Cradling the gun lovingly Jack jerked his head at Jim, "Come on! Let's go!" Within quarter of an hour they were up in the latest HeliMoth and accompanied by the usual bodyguard—two more HeliMoths with state of the art armament.

As they fluttered over Gene Control Jim felt a deep foreboding and gave an involuntary shudder at the strength of his feeling. Jack looked at him sharply with icy awareness, "Are you cold Jim?" His gimlet eyes seemed to plumb the depths of Jim's disloyal thoughts. *'Not at all, Jack—just an itch in the middle of my back.'* Jack lost interest as he caught sight of something through the window.

'What the hell—? Mike!' he yelled to one of the four accompanying armed police. "Go and ask the pilot if he recognises that Helimoth!" Jim had noticed the craft, but assumed it to be part of the entourage—nothing could surprise him now—he had seen the depths to which Government would sink. No expense would be spared to ensure the satisfactory amusement of ministers, or protect their financial interests. It had not seemed at all unusual that yet a third of these most expensive and latest craft should be used on the whim of his boss. Jack was shouting again, "There is no insignia—that Moth must be from Outside! Give chase!" The unknown Moth put on an amazing turn of speed, which Gene Control's latest could not match. It dwindled rapidly into the distance and behind a headland. For the next fifteen minutes they zoomed in and out of small deserted bays, everyone searching the beaches for activity. "I know what they're doing!" Jack was beside himself, "They're smuggling out Eternals. they must be stopped! Keep looking!" The hunting trip was forgotten, they were after a higher order of prey. Rounding another headland, in the distance Jim, at the rear of the Moth, caught sight of a group of people running across the sand like ants towards a grounded HeliMoth where they disappeared inside—then it seemed, in a few seconds, the same people leapt back out of the Moth and ran across the beach! He didn't say a word, hoping the runaways would escape, but pretended to scan the beach like everyone else praying no-one would notice. After about three minutes, just as the Moth took off from the beach Mike yelled, "There they are!" Jack bellowed, 'Fire! Shoot them down!" He and the guards hurried towards the cockpit. Jim looked at the gun Jack had shown him before their fight, which lay on the seat where his boss had been sitting. A moment's thought decided him—he snatched up the weapon and aimed at Jack, "Stop!" he called. "Let them go—people should be allowed to live where they like!" The guards raised their guns, "Drop it!" one of them ordered. Jim held his ground, Jack speechless and transfixed by the threatening weapon. "No!" said Jim, "You drop yours, otherwise the H.C.A. dies—and so do you!"

Jack screamed, "Drop your weapons! Drop your weapons—he means it—he'll kill us all!" One guard tightened his finger on the trigger and the laser burned a hole in the seat next to Jim as the other guard pushed down his partner's arm in an attempt to prevent Jim's retaliation. Without hesitating Jim fired a raking beam, which encompassed two of the four guards and the pilot's arm and destroyed the side of the Helimoth. There was not a lot of blood, because the laser effectively cauterised the wounds. Jack and the remaining guards had ducked to avoid the laser ('though Jack had sustained a slight wound to his arm—raised to protect his head as he ducked) and whilst they were still curled up behind the seats, Jim rushed to the front of the Helimoth, leaping over Jack's legs in passing; dived through the opening his laser had made and hurtled down into the sea without stopping to think of the consequences. The pilot, with gritted teeth was desperately trying to keep the moth on some kind of course. His left arm hung useless, almost severed at the elbow. The two who had escaped Jim's attack leapt up and fired at his rapidly disappearing body. One of the guards daringly suggested it might be a good idea if they all went to the hospital before Jack went to his office, which Jack grudgingly agreed to do)

Jim and the laser beams hit the water simultaneously, but mostly not in the same place. Unfortunately, just as he submerged he heard the water hiss and bubble and felt a searing pain in his left arm. It was a long way down, and by the time he surfaced, Jim's lungs were bursting. Fortunately he came up at some distance from his entry position having been dragged away by the current, so further shots missed him as the guards continued to fire at the position in which they had last seen him.

His (plastic) weapon surfaced nearby, and he used the waves to move towards it making small movements with his feet so as not to splash. Holding the water—proof gun along his body with his right arm, Jim breathed out and submerged kicking himself gently away from the area. He thanked God that the sun had almost set. With the fading light and small choppy waves breaking up the surface there was less likelihood of him being seen whilst submerged. Coming up occasionally for air he ended up about three hundred yards away to see the Moth wobbling its way erratically to the beach. He watched as it made a clumsy landing and tipped onto one side, the guards leaping out onto the beach and staggering away from the wreck. A small flame flickered on the fuselage followed by an explosion. The other Gene Control Moths were firing at the Outsiders, but their lasers seemed to have little effect—in fact as Jim watched, he saw laser beams reflect from their quarry to hit one of the pursuing Moths in its rotors, which caused it to spiral slowly but inexorably down into the sea. The other aggressor gave up, flew back to the beach, anti-gravved up the guards who had escaped the fire and took off over the headland. It was a long way to the beach and Jim didn't think he could make it. He could see the Outsiders' Moth hovering a few hundred yards away and waved frantically. 'They can't see me.' he thought, then realising he still had the laser weapon he pointed it into the air and fired a prolonged blast into the air.

CHAPTER 8

"They're shooting at us!" screamed Pam, "They're shooting at us!" Peter Marsden stood up. "Don't worry, everyone! Our Moth is more state of the art than theirs—we have a laser shield and they don't!" He addressed Malcolm and John, "Malcolm, you take charge of the laser, John adjust the shield if necessary—I'll watch out for casualties, we'll have to take them with us if necessary." Malcolm sounded amazed,

"That laser burst wasn't ours, it came from inside the government Moth—they must have an unwilling passenger." He fired several laser bursts.

Pam shouted excitedly, "Someone dived out of the government moth and they're shooting at him!"

"I can see him!" Michael pointed, "In the sea—there!" There was a loud hissing crash, as a shot from one of the supporting Moths ricocheted and returned to its origin.

"Hooray! The biter bit!" Pogie yelled. They watched as the damaged Moth fell into the sea. The remaining Government moth picked up the guards from the beach and swiftly disappeared over the headland.

The pilot rotored down and anti-gravved Jim from the sea. Water poured from him as he hovered in the antigrav beam. Unable to climb in on his own, Jim felt eager hands grab his soaking clothes and soon lay gasping on the carpeted floor of the Outside Moth.

"Medic!" called Peter, kneeling by Jim, "We have a wounded man here. Your name sir"?

"Jim Speke. Minister—."

"I know—for Subject Control. We know all about you! Your arm looks bad—but don't worry—you probably don't believe it, but our technology is more advanced than Gene Control's!" Two medics worked together, cutting away clothing from Jim's arm and encapsulating it in a very unusual dressing with a solid, translucent cover. All pain was immediately relieved. Wet clothes removed and dressed in clean overalls, Jim was still coughing and spluttering and trying to thank them at the same time, "Thank hu-huhu y-huhuhuo!"

"Don't try to thank us yet—there's plenty of time now." Marsden paused, and looked at Malcolm, "We have a Government Minister here, Malcolm!"

Two medics worked together, cutting away clothing from Jim's arm and encapsulating it in a very unusual dressing with a solid, translucent cover. All pain was immediately relieved. Wet clothes removed and wrapped in warm covers, Jim was given a hot drink (When they finally landed at the heliport in 'Advance'—Outside's capital city, everyone wanted to talk to him and wish him well as he had made a great contribution to the defeat of the government forces which had threatened them).

As the Government Moths had all now left the area (or ditched in the sea!), Malcolm stashed the laser and went over to Jim. The medics had taken away the first aid equipment, and he was now safely ensconced in a reclining seat. Malcolm took him by his free hand and gently shook it. "Yes!" he said, "I've seen you on television Sir. That was a very brave thing you did. We are very grateful for your help, if you had not helped us we could have been killed—including these children and their parents we were rescuing from Gene Control!"

These children, had been watching wide-eyed the spectacle of Jim being rescued from the sea, Jim now settled in a seat, they lost interest and started to look around them. "Where are we going?" asked Pam. "Yes!" Chorused Michael and Sarah, "Where *are* we going?" Ian popped his head round the seat of and whispered, "We're going 'Outside'! Play some games for a while, and then go to sleep. It will be a long time before we get there!" Michael touched his hand, "Okay Dad!" he said.

It was beginning to get dark when Sarah, sitting by the window, started in surprise. She nudged Michael with her elbow and whispered, "*Look Michael! In the forest! PEOPLE!*" Michael leaned across her lap, half kneeling on his seat, their heads almost touching. "Where?" he said. "no—oh—Oh yes! I just got a glimpse!" they both kept looking for a few seconds, then Michael flopped back into his seat. Sarah stared at him expectantly, finally she whispered impatiently, "*What did you see?*"

"*Well,*" Michael also whispered, "*I thought—no, there were people in that gap in the trees—weren't there?*"

"*Yes! I saw them too! I thought the forest only had wild animals in it—didn't you?" "Yes." They sat tensely, looking at each other, both frowning slightly. Sarah relaxed, still looking at her brother, "Perhaps we should say something—what do you think?" "Not now," said Michael, "wait until we get to Advance." "Okay!"* They relaxed. The sun was about to set and the forest was looking increasingly gloomy and dark against the brilliance of the sunset—soon it would be night. Half asleep they heard Pogie ask, "How long before we get there?" Someone answered, "you might as well have a sleep—it will be quite a while! If you're not tired, there are computer games, films to watch—or there is a short history of Outside if you're interested—touch number one on the screen."

Sarah awoke suddenly, opened her eyes and stretched, suddenly conscious of a hushed bustling around her. It was still dark outside. The moth had landed and the crew was sorting out, opening and closing storage places and luggage compartments. Their parents were talking quietly behind them. Michael stretched and started to speak, rubbing his eyes, "Are we there?" "Yes, we've landed! I can't see much—we're on top of a building and all I can see is the top of the roof and a circle of light." Sarah's nose was pressed to the window.

Marsden walked up to their parents, "Good morning!" he said. "Your luggage has been taken to your hotel room and the Hover-bug is waiting to whisk you and their children to the hotel. There is plenty of time for you to refresh yourselves before breakfast (Buttle is there to serve you!), after which I shall guide you to reception. I will see you later."

Katy said, "Thank you Peter!" Then, "Did you hear that Ian? Buttle will be there! I thought we had left him at home?" Ian put his arm around her,

"Don't you remember? They told us they had cloned him, so that we would still have him as part of our life in Outside, and the authorities would be unaware of our disappearance (with the clones of ourselves there too) for long enough to give us time to escape".

Katy laughed, I wonder what they will make of 'us' still being at home!"

"They'll hopefully think at first that *we* are the clones and the real people are at Gene Control and that the Outsiders have failed in their bid to rescue us. But of course, they will eventually realise that is not the case. Oh! I think we're getting off—come on my Love".

PART NINE

Jack was furious! The HCA stormed from the Moth, shouting. "That's IT! I'm going to declare WAR on Outside!' I won't have them interfering and taking our subjects away!" The Pilot had called for help to Gene Control, who put the Moth onto Main Beam and whisked it straight back to base. It had not been on main beam previously, because there was no specific route for random journeys such as that undertaken by ministers on outings, or staff looking for escapees.

Two of the remaining staff had anaesthetized his arm and encased it in protective dressing (treated the pilot's arm likewise—and now carrying him on a stretcher). The adrenaline stopped flowing Jack realised his arms still hurt and followed his staff to the lift, and thence to the hospital, where suitably calming injections were given in to all those who had suffered from the trauma.

CHAPTER 9

The hotel suite was magnificent Katy stared open mouthed. "How could Gene Control tell us Outside was primitive? Just look at that furniture!" She sank into a blue seat, which immediately moulded itself to her body, "O_O_OH! It's so comfortable."

Pogie, Pam, Sarah and Michael could be heard (at least, the 'woosh' of doors could) as they rushed from room to room exclaiming in delight at all the new technology. Somewhere, someone had turned on TV. "Wow! Look at this! It's 3D virtual reality—you can walk in!"

Katy called out, "Come here please, all of you! We must get ready to meet the family!" As every bedroom (three of them) had a grooming station, everyone was soon ready, getting clean clothes from the case. The new state of the art Buttle was greeted with delight as Michael and Sarah found him, serving breakfast in the dining area. As they ate, the viewing screen was activated. "Good morning! I hope you're enjoying breakfast!" Marsden beamed from the screen, 'when you're ready, there is a link to the Portaway in the vestibule—press the open button, walk in and you will be taken down to it. Then you will be transported to the meeting place. See you later!"

Breakfast was rather hurried, but it was great having Buttle to look after them again, "It's going to be ok here!" spluttered Michael, through his favourite breakfast cereal. "Don't stop to talk!" said Katy, "it's going to be a very busy day, and we need to be quick—**without** rushing!" she admonished Michael, who had started to shovel in the cereal with indecent haste! Dressed, fed and excited, the children hugged Buttle, and followed Katy and Ian out of the hotel to a waiting Hoverbus, where Peter Marsden was waiting to greet them. "I love going up in the antigrav!" said Sarah to Marsden, as he ushered her to the opening where she was sucked gently up into the bus. Just as Michael was about to do the same, someone must have knocked the switch, because instead of being sucked upwards, he was (gently!) pinned to the ground. Marsden called up,

"The passengers are *entering*, not leaving!" "Oops! Sorry sir!' and the Antigrav was reversed.

"There's your grandmother!" Katy pointed from the hoverbus transporting them. Michael and Sarah leaned across eagerly, but there were so many people waiting—cameras pointed at the moth or waving furiously—it was impossible to tell where their grandmother was! "We don't know what she looks like!" they chorused. The bus hovered gently near the crowd and passengers began to antigrav out, "Don't worry—she'll be hugging you both in a minute!" Katy waved frantically, then turned to see what was the hold-up.

"Come along!" Marsden said, holding out his hand to Pogie, who had stopped near the antigrav, "Where's the dome for Outside?" he asked. Ian smiled, "There is no dome for Outside, Pogie—that's why it's called 'Outside', because it's completely outside!"

"Wow!" said Pam, looking over Pogie's shoulder, "That means every time it rains we'll get wet if we don't get home in time!"

"Yes—you've got it! If you're not indoors you are always exposed to whatever the weather is doing. No one is going to tell you that it will rain at 2 o'clock precisely (or, as at Gene Control, at night so that you are safely in bed!)." Sarah and Michael were already hurrying over to their mother as Marsden helped the twins into the antigrav, which lowered them smoothly to the ground. They shouted their thanks hurriedly and rushed after their friends.

Ian hesitated, aware that he would probably never again see all the people and friends he had known at Gene Control—and wondering what work he would do Outside. He suddenly felt very alone and turned to Marsden, "Are you coming with us?" he asked. "No Ian. Our job is over once you are on the ground."

"Well, thank you very much on everyone's behalf for rescuing us". Marsden took Ian's proffered hand and shook it vigorously.

"It's been a pleasure, Ian. Don't worry, we shall meet again! You are very important to Security, having worked at Gene Control! Go and meet your family, have a good holiday and get used to Outside—I shall get in touch later to see how you've settled—we shall probably need you in Security! See you soon!"

"I look forward to that." Comforted, Ian walked eagerly towards the crowd.

PART TEN

Jack had calmed down considerably. The helimoth pilot and the other injured crew members were in hospital having limbs replaced where necessary. Thought raced through the HCA's head. *'I'd better not declare war on Outside just yet—better check up on the state of their weaponry...'* He touched the screen: O.D.S responded at once. All further correspondence was in code.

CHAPTER 10

Katy grabbed Michael and Sarah's hands, 'Come on you two—I can see your Grandma!' A small slim figure darted out of the crowd and rushed towards them, 'Katy! My darling—how wonderful to see you after all these years!' Her last words were muffled in Katy's hair as they hugged for what, to the children, seemed ages. Finally, they came up for air, and Andrea held out her arms to the children Sarah and Michael walked towards her to be enveloped in her loving arms, Andrea, her hands still gripping their arms as though she would never let go, moved back to look at their faces. "I thought I may never see you!" she said. "What lovely children you are—my grandchildren!"

"Hello Grandma!" said Michael, "I've heard a lot about you from Mum!" Andrea laughed, "I expect you have! But I don't even know your names yet!" "I'm Michael and this is Sarah."

"How pretty you are, Sarah—I hope we shall have some lovely times together now you're here."

"Hallo Grandma!" Sarah as they returned her hug. "Oh! Are these two yours as well Katy?" Mrs. Stevens released her grandchildren and hedl out her arms to Pogie and Pam, who had just caught up and were standing back, not quite sure what to do. Katy put her arms around their shoulders and introduced them, "They are children of friends of ours—Tom and Jaimie—we hope they will be able to join us later." Mrs. Stevens gave the twins a hug too, then pulled back to look at them, "As far as I am concerned, you are both part of this family and will be very welcome in my house, Pogie and Pam! We shall make every effort to find your parents."

A look passed between Katy and Andrea, who realized at once that there was a problem which should not be spoken of in front of the children! "Well, Pogie and Pam, come and have a hug—you shall be part of this family until your parents are able to escape. I have a lovely big house where there is plenty of room for all of you until you decide where you want to live." She stood up. "I hope you don't mind, but I decided not to throw a big party yet. I thought you'd all be needing a rest, Katy, until you get used to Outside—is that alright with you?"

"Mum, of course it's alright! We can always have a party later, when we have got used to being outside and the children have found new friends. You haven't said hallo to Ian yet—this is my lovely husband."

"Oh Ian! I'm so sorry—I was so excited to see Katy and the children—I didn't mean to leave you out." She held out her arms and Ian hugged her, lifting her off her feet and laughing, "Don't worry about it!" he said, "This is the first time we have met—how could you recognize me? It's good to meet you—and to be 'Outside'!"

"Well! How are you getting on?" Peter Marsden arrived and put an arm around Mrs. Stevens It must be good to see your family he said, smiling. "Well! I'm glad we made it Ian!" he said, "-thanks of course to Jim Speke!" "Where is he?" Katy asked.

"He's been taken to hospital for treatment,—and of course, he'll be bringing Outside Security up-to date on developments at Gene Control—then he will be found lodgings". Katy turned to Ian, "He's going to be all on his own Ian! It seems wrong after all he did for us. Do you think we could have him to stay with us for a while until he finds his feet here?—Of course—if that's alright with you Mother! I am assuming that we shall be allowed to go to my Mother's house, Peter?"

"Of *course* you may go to your Mother's house—all the necessary checks no you were carried out before we rescued you. As to what will happen to Jim Speke—that will have to wait until Clearance has made the necessary checks on him—after all, he has been a member of the Gene Control government for some time, and we can't risk any sabotage, or information about Outside matters to get back to the Head of Combined Affairs—Jack Dickinson is notorious for his violent nature, and the last thing we need is for him to get control of Outside as well as Gene Control. If he were let loose on genetic modification of plants 'Outside', there would be famine and mayhem—I know what happened in the past—and he's still got that bee in his bonnet!

At the moment, all modified plant material is confined in the Domes in secret stores—if they should contaminate 'Outside', the World would be in considerable trouble! It was bad enough before Gene Control went under cover, it took years before all growing modified plants were, thankfully, destroyed—but even then, we had to feed the third world for years (when modified plants there failed to produce crops) before they were able to manage on their own!"

"Really?" said Katy, "I didn't know that!" Ian nodded, "Yes. I heard rumours about that, a couple of centuries ago, but we didn't know whether to believe them or not."

Marsden raised his eyebrows, "Interesting. It's surprising that food was successfully grown in Gene Control!"

"I never saw genetically modified seeds being sold," said Ian,—many of us grew our own vegetables and used the seeds from them to grow more the following year—we used hydroponics of course."

Marsden was angry, "They must have kept the genetically modified plant material stored away somewhere safe—that's typical of Gene Control—to leave people to starve to death through their mistakes—*and* to keep hold of the very cause of the famine! You see why those in the know decided to leave and go Outside!

Anyway we waste time—your luggage will be collected for you and delivered to Andrea's house—I presume your cases etc are still packed? Katy nodded. I'll say 'Goodbye' then. I shall see you later Ian, when you start work with us," Peter began to shake hands all round or hug as appropriate, then the family followed Andrea to the transporter.

It was warm and sunny outside, but the wind was blowing quite strongly. "What a strong wind!" gasped Sarah, "It was never this strong in Gene Control!" Pam giggled, "It's a good job we're wearing trousers Sarah—I think I'll be wearing trousers all the time here!"

"Come along everyone—I can't wait to get you all home!" Andrea clicked her fingers and a nearby transporter opened for loading, sucking the luggage into an expandable boot, which sealed itself on completion with no evidence of an opening. Pogie stared, "That's amazing!" he said—, "we don't have that in Gene Control!" Andrea ushered them into the vehicle and with a wave of her hands arranged the seats so they could all see each other. "Who's going to drive?" asked Michael. "No-one!" laughed Andrea, "—it's programmed to go home and park in the garage!" "What—without a Travel beam?" chorused Pogie and Michael. "Of course." nodded Andrea contentedly. The boys looked at each other and shrugged, "It looks as though the technology here is better than in Gene Control Pogie!" "Yes!" Pogie said, "It's going to be fine here—at least, it would be if Mum and Dad were with us." A table rose up between them with a screen in front of each person, "Which game would you like to play? Click on the one you like best, and the computer will bring up the most popular one!" There was time to play more than one game—Outside was much bigger than Gene control!

* * *

After a few days relaxation, Ian started work with Peter and his team. Before he went, he impressed upon the children that they must follow the rules given to them by Peter Marsden and not go near the river or the forest—both of which were extremely dangerous. Until they had been to school for a few weeks, he preferred that they stay in the grounds belonging to their grandmother's house—there was plenty of space to build dens, and there was a small stream which they could dam to make a pool if they liked—Andrea was in complete agreement and showed them where they could get materials and equipment to re-create their private places, just as they had in Gene Control.

By the time the den was finished and the pool was almost full, with an outflow opened so that fish could survive above and below the dam, the holiday was over—it was time for the children to start school. Within a few weeks they were into a routine, had made friends with other children and found out which teachers were 'pupil friendly'—Mr. Merton was one to look out for—he believed that all children were constantly up to mischief and could not be trusted to do as they were told. If he had known that the four from Gene Control were planning to make a raft; tether it to trees near the river and float on it, he would have had them confined to the house for the whole holiday. As it was, they had to keep lookout for him, as he often walked past Andrea's house and might have seen them sneaking away to the river, which they already had managed quite frequently without anyone finding out. Weekends were free for children to do as they liked—within reason!

Pogie and Michael had stashed away construction equipment (saws; strong twine; axes; knives—any tools which they might need for chopping down tress and sawing logs—plus waterproof material for protecting it all in case of rain). Working amongst trees as they did by the river, was reminiscent of their holiday work in the wooded area of Gene Control where they had built the little wattle and daub den. They were enjoying the unpredictable weather and learning how to cope with it—been soaked in a thunderstorm and suffered severe thirst when they forgot to take water in a drought! They realized later that they could have boiled water from the river, "Only if we had a saucepan!" Pointed out Sarah. They already knew how to make a fire safely, ensuring that it couldn't set fire to anything nearby.

The raft was finished well before the summer term ended, they had even managed to float it and retrieve it with the ropes which tethered it to the trees. Getting on the raft was not easy without getting wet—both Pogie and Sarah had fallen in the river the first time—they were very late home that day, as they had to dry the wet clothes by the fire and get them as flat as possible—and of course, to get into the house without anyone noticing! Then the clothes were put in with the dirty washing, and as it was so late, all the children changed into their night clothes.

"What? Ready for bed already?" commented Ian, "Aren't you going to have dinner—we've saved you some?" Pogie answered quickly, "We had a picnic—took a lot of food with us." "Anyway," Michael put in, "we were so late—it's almost time for supper!"

Ian looked at his watch, "So it is!" he said in surprise. Pleadingly, Sarah asked "Please can we watch 3Dteevee?"

Katy came in, "We've saved you dinner—it's keeping warm!" "They say they had a picnic." Ian informed her. "Well, you'll have to eat it for supper!" said Katy, firmly.

*   *   *

Next day was the first day of the summer holiday, and the four youngsters couldn't wait to get back to the raft. They did the chores as quickly as possible—clearing the breakfast table, washing up and sorting the trash (Buttle was still being reprogrammed at the Robot Centre, so someone had to take over for a while and the children got the job—Grandma had never used a robot and wasn't sure she wanted one!) - Katy was amazed when they went to her and asked if they could go out. 'That was so quick! I've never known you to be so quick—why are you in such a hurry?'

'We're meeting some of our friends and if we're late they'll go off exploring without us!'

'Off you go then—don't go in the river and keep away from THE FOREST!' Katy called after them—glad they were settling in so well.

'Ok Mum!' chorused Michael and Sarah and 'Okay Katy!' yelled Pogie and Pam, as the doors slid to behind them.

Children were ever expert in avoiding supervision and getting up to mischief and Pogie, Pam, Michael and Sarah were no exception. There were things about Gene control which they missed—the dens in the 'forest' they had used for years—the safe water sports in the artificial lake and evenly flowing river and they had a quiet unspoken determination to test the exhilarating wilderness of this new situation. Not only had they constructed the raft and enjoyed having it out on the river for the first time, Michael had already studied maps of the area in the school library and knew that the river past through a narrow channel between high cliffs then through a hilly area ending up lower down in the forest—where it went after that he had as yet no idea. Still as long as the raft was finished and tethered, they could still practise their rowing against the current, paddling back and then letting raft go again and so on—the girls had had a go as well, although not being as strong as the boys they found it difficult to paddle against the current.

Avoiding supervision was not so easy now, as Mr. Merton, the history and science teacher, lived fairly close to their grandmother. Consequently, they were often meeting him around unexpected corners on school-free days and had to take care not to be going too fast!

They couldn't wait to get to the river and start paddling. They had often practised zooming around the roads and the occasional houses which were well spaced each with vegetable gardens, flowerbeds and grassed and wooded areas—so they grabbed their hover boards and zoomed off down the road. Suddenly, "Watch out!" Pogie yelled, "I can see Mr. Merton!"

In the distance a lanky figure strode towards them. "Press your deceleration buttons!" By the time they reached their teacher the four were floating sedately along. "Good morning Sir!" they chorused. Mr. Merton stopped, "—and where are you off to today?" The teacher raised one eyebrow suspiciously—he never trusted children. "Just exploring Sir!" They chorused. "Make sure you don't go near the river! It is *not* safe—and you're not in Gene Control now you know." "Yes Sir," they chorused, in noncommittal, ambiguous agreement, "goodbye Mr. Merton!" they continued sedately on their way, itching to speed up, but waiting until 'Sir' was a safe distance away!

The terrain here was flat and in places you could be seen from a long way off, but as the houses ended there was a shrub eerier with occasional small groups of trees. It was early morning and Mr. Merton fortunately turned out to be the only person about. They chased each other over bushes on the way to—what else? THE RIVER! Today they were all wearing swimwear under their clothes. The sun beamed from the deep blue sky and a gentle breeze ruffled their hair. "Oh! I love it Outside," called Sarah. "So do I!" Pam swerved to avoid a rabbit which jumped up in fear as she passed overhead. "Me too-oo! Yahoo-oo!" yelled Pogie, soaring into the air over a bush. "Come on! Let's get to the river!" Michael rapidly shrank from sight as he switched to maximum. Yelling in exhilaration the other three sped after him.

Sunlight glinted and sparkled off the rippling water, an otter plopped in and swam away as they drew up on the riverbank by the copse, leaving a V-shaped wake as he swam away. The children picked up their boards and squeezed between the trees to the hidden hollow where the boys had made and concealed the raft. They had managed to acquire more tools—just as up-to-date as those they had at Gene control (their school equipment) with which they were allowed to practice during vacation. Now they used tools found in the garage—and borrowed them. The raft was quite well made—The copse had been deprived of about eight trees with suitable sturdy trunks, not fully grown—but easier to manage than mature trees. Twine and rope had also been acquired from the garage and each six-foot length of trunk tightly bound to its neighbour in seven places, with extra lengths of twine and rope for tethering loops at each end. A mast had been considered, but decided against, as they had no tools to cope with fitting it to the raft—and questions would have been asked if they wanted to borrow those! Four paddles had been fashioned from the unused parts of the trunks—one each for the children and four spares fastened to the ropes joining the trunks. There was a tethering rope on each corner, plus a paddle attached with twine and four stabilising trunks across and underneath the raft.

"I will check the tethering ropes!" called Pogie, after they'd uncovered and checked over the raft. He looked at the ropes carefully, they seem to be okay, the knots were tight (unfortunately, he did not check behind the trunks, where a nosy rodent of some kind had chewed both ropes, but not quite right through! Sarah and Pam climbed onto the raft—one at each end to balance it, and the boys pushed it out onto the river, leaping on to it at the last minute as it floated gently into the current across the shallow, calm water near the bank. It was quite safe, they thought, and they could now practise paddling backwards against the current, which they had already done several times previously. It was so good to work and play in the fresh air!

The raft gathered speed with the current, no need to paddle at first—just to steer, taking it in turns to follow Michael's orders of, 'left back—front right' etc. Michael was quickest at knowing which oar doing what, would steer the raft in the right direction. They quickly reached the end of the tethers and proceeded to paddle hard against the current to take the raft back to base. Behind the trees, the gnawed strands of the rope began to fray and one by one the remaining strands parted company. The front row parted first and slipped into the water, making the front of the raft swing to the left. "The rope's come undone," shouted Sarah, gathering it in, "it's all chewed and frayed!" she said, looking at the end. "Good job we used two tethers!" Sarah caught hold of the remaining tether and hauled them backwards.

It was just beginning to work, the raft moving slowly back against the current, when the other tether broke! Pam screamed, "Oh no, the rope's broken!" Paddling furiously, Michael shouted, "I thought you checked the tethers Pogie?"

"I did!" Pogie shouted back, "-they looked fine to me—completely intact!"

"Just keep paddling!" Michael yelled, "try to get upstream above the tethering place, so we can guide it to the bank with the current!" There was silence apart from the rushing water, heavy breathing and splashing paddles. They tried hard, but the raft stayed where it was. "I can't do this much longer!" panted Sarah. "You'd better try!" gasped Michael. "Otherwise, I don't know where we shall end up!" They were all facing backwards, wet paddles flashing in the sun, "I think we shall end up in the forest," shouted Pogie, "it goes through the forest—the river!" Sarah and Pam screamed together, "Oh! No-oo!" They paddled furiously.

There was a fraught silence, as each child used every atom of strength to get back to shore—in vain. "Okay everyone—give up paddling. Try to steer to the bank before we reach the part between the cliffs. If we do get there, just try to keep us away from the rocks!" The current increased and the raft started to turn, "Left back! Right front!" Michael frantically shouted instructions, "All oars in—paddle as fast as you can!" The orders came fast and furious as the high cliffs sped past and petered out. The river widened as the cliffs dwindled away behind them and the current slowed. "Let's try to get to the bank—the right bank—before the forest starts". Pogie began paddling towards the bank. "Yes," said Michael, "we'll have to leave the raft here and walk back over the cliffs."

There was a fierce and a current, which inexorably swung them to the left bank as they struggled and concentrated fiercely on their task, trees appeared on both sides of the river. The forest gradually thickened as the current slowed, "There's a man on the bank!" shouted Pogie, but by the time everyone turned to look, "No!—he's gone!" Pogie sounded relieved. The raft slowed right down, the forest was becoming dark and threatening on either side of the river. Voices sounded amongst the trees, words indecipherable, but angry. They caught glimpses of people in gaps between the trees. "Uh—oh!" said Michael, "there's a beach ahead." Sure enough the bank curved outward to their right, and a sandy area edged by rocks bulged out into the river. Worse! There were men on the rocks and beach—very wild looking men—with sticks! They were almost naked and with flowing unkempt hair.

"Paddle right!" yelled Michael, "—try not to land on the beach!" They managed to get around the rocks, but there were men in the water—two of them leapt onto the raft and grabbed Sarah and Pogie and two others grabbed hold of the ropes and yanked the raft between the rocks onto the beach! 'Spies from Gene Control!' yelled a voice. 'YES! Take them to the Boss!' Two men to each child, they were dragged, protesting, through the trees and brambles. "We're NOT from Gene Control!" yelled Sarah. "No! We're from Outside!" Yelled Michael and Pogie. "We escaped—the Robot people from Outside helped us to escape!" panted Sarah. The forest people had never heard of the robots. One of the men shouted at the children angrily, "You've been shooting at us! We saw your helimoth only last week! Two people got shot—one is dead and you took the other away!" "Honestly, it wasn't us!" said Pogie.

"Shut-up!" said one of the men—and hit Pogie on the head with a stick. "OUCH!" said Pogie, and tried to put his hand on the sore place, but the men kept tight hold of him.

The children did not try to speak again, but allowed the men to rush them along, deeper into the forest. Thorns tore at their clothes and scratched their skin and branched whipped their faces as their captors dragged them along. Pam began to cry—all the pent up emotion from her father's attack on their mum and the loss of both parents taking over. Sarah saw her crying. "Don't be so horrible to us!" she screamed, "Gene Control has killed her Dad, and she's lost her Mum!" Only one of the men heard what she said—he stopped and took Pam from the other man, picked her up and began to carry her. "What are you doing?" bellowed the other man, "They're spies!" "They're a bit young for that, don't you think?" said his fellow. The shouting man shut up and followed, grumpily chuntering and complaining as they moved along.

At last they came out into a space in the trees, where small domed buildings woven from branches and plastered with mud stood around the clearing. A larger, square shelter stood amongst them, where a man sat on a stump with a large staff in his right hand. The children were dragged in front of him and roughly thrown to the ground, except Pam, who was still sobbing on her captor's shoulder. The leader of the men who had first grabbed the raft yelled at the top of his voice. **'Boss! Boss! Spies—from Gene Control!'** The other men began to chant in loud voices, 'SPIES! SPIES! SPIES!'

"Then kill them!" said the boss. Two men grabbed hold of Michael. They only had one knife between them and began to fight for it, dropping him in the process. He ran forward and knelt in front of the Boss. "Please sir, we were rescued from Gene Control and now we live Outside." The boss stared at him. Another man rushed forward and tried to grab Michael—"Leave him!" shouted the Boss, "let him have his say!" he looked down at Michael, "Stand-up boy!" he growled. Michael stood—and (pointing as he spoke) gabbled—, "—this is Pogie, that is Pam. Their Dad attacked their Mum and was taken to the Gene Control Laboratory and executed. I think their mum died. When we escaped, my mum and dad took Pogie and Pam with us to be looked after. We don't want to be kept young anymore, we just want to grow up!"

Pam looked up her face wet with tears, "I just want my mum!" she sobbed. Some women had come out of the small domed buildings. One of them came over and stood by the boss. "Pam?" she said, amazement showing in her face, "Is that really you?" Everyone looked at the woman. Pam wiped away the tears on her sleeves and rubbed her eyes. She stared at the Lady incredulously. "Muuu-um!" she screamed, "Muuu-um!" and rushed towards the lady with her arms out. All the men moved out of the way as Jamie Mailer ran forward and picked up her daughter, hugging her tightly and smothering her with kisses. "MUM!" yelled Pogie. His captors released him too, and watched as the three hugged each other with tears running down their cheeks.

The Boss stood up, "Well!" he said, "I think we have proof that these children are not Spies! If they are not, then perhaps Gene Control were lying when they said there was no such thing as a civilisation called 'OUTSIDE'!—or that we would catch dangerous diseases if we passed the forest. Perhaps we should send someone to look. The children may be able to show us the way—what do you all think?" There was a muttered discussion amongst the wild men. Most of them nodded and one said, "We agree! Let's investigate—we need civilization!"

Michael stepped forward, "I'm sure Outside will send transport to take you there—and find you all somewhere to live—they did it for us!"

"What is your name, boy?" asked the Boss.

"Michael, Sir," he said politely.

The Boss stood up and banged his staff on the ground. "Everyone to the Meeting Hall!" He turned and led the way, followed by the now silent men and the women—more of whom had come out of the huts to see what was going on. In the 'Hall', everyone sat on tree—stumps arranged in rows, Sarah, Pogie and Pam and their Mum at the front. The Boss's stump was on a flattened grassy hump of ground, like a small stage. "Stand here, Michael!" said the Boss, indicating a spot near his seat on the 'stage'. "Please tell us everything."

Michael talked about their life at Gene Control; Buttle—especially how he saved Michael from the men from Gene Control he found in their house; their den in the 'forest'; the demonstrations about growing up—and most of all, how they escaped and how wonderful it was Outside! "The people there build houses for you if you've nowhere to go—and there's a hostel for you to live in until your house is ready. Your children can go to school, and the only difference between Outside and Gene Control, is that you have more freedom!"

"What about the roads?" someone called out, "-have they got Autohover?"

"Yes!" said Michael, smiling, "You can use autohover if you want, or just drive yourself—as long as you don't drive over other people's private property—you can cut across open country if you know your way about, but you have to have the beam turned on in case you get lost and need help!" The people looked at each other and there was a buzz of conversation, "It sounds good to me!" called out one man. Everyone nodded, and snatches of remarks could be heard, "Sounds good—,"

"—lovely to live in a proper house." The Boss held up his hand, "Let Michael finish before we talk about it!" he said. Michael finished by telling them of the robot repairer from Outside, who had look-alike robots made of all of them, so that Gene Control would not know they had gone until well after they had escaped.

A voice from the audience said, "I think you should go and look first, Boss and make sure it's how the boy says." Michael said, "You don't have to stay if you don't want—they will bring you back to the forest!" A lady stood up, "We have no way of getting in touch with Outside!" Pogy stood up, "I've got a communicator!" he said, "children are supposed to carry them everywhere in case they get lost!"

"Have you all got them?" asked someone else. Michael hesitated, then explained, "I left mine in the copse where we made the raft!" he confessed—"So did we!" confessed Sarah and Pam. Michael, looking sheepish said, "We're supposed to have them with us all the time, but we thought they might get lost in the water." Everyone laughed, and a voice said, "Well! That's proof that they are only children—and that they are telling us the truth!" Everyone nodded. "Shall I call Outside?" asked Pogie. The Boss stood up, "How about it everyone? Do you feel happy about going to Outside? Shall we let—what's your name boy?"

"Everyone calls me Pogie!" he said.

"Fine! Call them up and tell them all about it, Pogie!" said the Boss, sitting down again.

Pogie called Marsden and explained where they were. Marsden was angry at first—"I thought you four were responsible people! Whatever possessed you to play on the river—you know how dangerous it is!" Pogie started to apologise, but Marsden cut him short, "At least you had your communicators with you!" Pogie pulled a scared face at the others, but he didn't let on that the others had no communicators with them. The Boss spoke, "Let me speak to the man in charge, please Pogie." Pogie handed the gadget to the Boss, who had a brief conversation with Marsden, then the boss handed back the gadget to Pogie and said, "Mr. Marsden says you must keep this turned on, and they will use it to find us. He knows about the beach, and they will try to land there—it will take about an hour—he thinks he has already found the site on an old map!"

Someone stood up, and said, "Why don't we all go to the beach and wait? It's sunny and warm!"

"Right!" Said the Boss, "If anyone has anything they need to take with them, fetch it now—because I don't think we'll be coming back!"

The Transporters (accompanied by protective, armed Airfloats—unknown to Gene control—with technology far in advance of that in the Helimoths, in case of aggression by Gene Control) silently arrived and set down safely on the beach. First to alight were armed soldiers, weapons at the ready and aimed at the waiting refugees—Peter Marsden was taking no chances! Michael and Sarah rushed out to meet him—ready with their excuses and apologies for going on the river. "Mr. Marsden! We're so sorry— Mr. Marsden—look who we found!" they chorused. Marsden interrupted them, "Don't worry, you two! We're only too glad we found you! Where is the Boss you tell me about?" The twins introduced the two men, who shook hands, Marsden's left hand on the Boss's shoulder, "Good to meet you Sir!" Marsden shook the boss's hand firmly, "What is your name?"

"It's so long since I used it—I've almost forgotten it!" Laughed the Boss, relieved and happy to be greeted so politely, "It's James Parrot. I used to work for Gene Control—they were going to get rid of me, but I was warned, and escaped before they came for me!"

"Oh! Yes! We heard about you—wondered if you were hiding in the forest—now—to business, let's get everyone on board and back to Outside and safety." Before he could issue any more instructions a soldier brought a message from the pilot in charge of the mission, "Sir!" said the soldier, saluting. "The Pilot has something on the detector—there may be G.C. helimoths in the vicinity." Marsden reacted immediately, "EVERYONE TAKE COVER!"

PART ELEVEN

Jack was feeling much better. His arm was healing nicely; however, he was still very miffed about Jim's defection to Outside, and needed to vent his rage upon anyone suitable. He called to his secretary, "Buck?" Buck appeared at the door, blonde hair ruffled, eyebrows raised, "Yes Sir?" "How do you fancy a shooting trip?" "Really Sir?" Overcome at the honour of being invited to join in—Buck was speechless for the moment. "Well?" Jack was even more miffed at the hesitation of such a lowly minion to accept his offer. "Perhaps you'd rather I asked someone else?" "Oh! No Sir! I'd be delighted to accompany you—thank you very much for asking me!" he groveled.

"Get a couple of weapons from supplies—and meet me at the Heliramp in—say—20 minutes—oh, and don't forget to get yourself some suitable gear from stores!" "Yes SIR! I'll go now!"

Duly armed, with a spare EMR weapon and suitably attired, Buck met his superior at the Heliramp, where they beamed up into the moth where the crew waited.

CHAPTER 11

Arriving at the forest, the crew, Jack and Buck (apart from the guards who would stay to watch over the helimoths) were set down in a clearing. "What game are we looking for Sir?" asked Buck innocently. Jack looked at him sternly, "We are looking for traitors to Gene Control—that is the 'game' we are aiming for!" Buck was shocked,

"What? *PEOPLE?*" He blurted, suddenly realising what he had let himself in for—he had thought to be shooting pheasants or ducks perhaps foxes—not people! "Precisely!" snapped Jack with a determined nod of his head, "Keep your eyes peeled—there are plenty of them here." Jack stomped off ahead, leaving Buck and his usual shooting party to follow through the brambles and thickets. After about ten minutes he stopped, "I can't understand it,—we've usually seen someone by now—where are they all?" He pondered, then, "I know where their living quarters are—saw them on a reconnaissance a few weeks ago. I'll just put the moth crew on red alert—we might need back-up!" He called the Moth. "Captain? You're on red alert—be ready to provide back-up. We're going to the Runners' head-quarters on the river bend. Over and Out. This way, Buck." Buck followed his Boss through the thickets and glades. He could hear water gurgling and trickling somewhere ahead of them. (*'Must be the river.'*) He thought.

"This way! It's near the river." Off they set, the undergrowth getting thicker as they went. Buck caught his jacket on something and heard it rip, but Jack was steaming ahead, the accompanying soldiers spread out around him—they were used to it—although they had never been quite so far into the forest on foot before, only viewing the area from the air.

A message came through the chip in Jack's ear, "Sir! I can see the beach. It's about 500 yards from your present position. Sending image to all." (Apart from Buck, everyone who had been on the hunting trips before, was fitted with the latest technology—chips and viewing technology implanted in their heads).

"Well done!" said Jack, "—we'll be with you shortly."

5 minutes later Jack's team erupted roaring and shooting onto the beach—only to be immediately immobilized by Outside's superior control technology—including the bullets—stopped in mid trajectory, they fell useless to the sandy ground!

The Runners, children and Outsiders stepped out of their hiding places amongst the trees and bushes. Even if he wanted to, Jack was unable to call up the helimoths, as the invisible controls allowed no escape. They watched helplessly, as Marsden and his team rounded up the refugees and the children who had found them and directed them onto the transporters. Don't worry about bringing clothes or possessions (unless you managed to bring anything valuable out of Gene Control!). Every thing you need will be provided by Outside Management. Only one or two of the refugees had valuables to take with them, and by the time those had been rescued, everyone was sitting comfortably in the transporters. Michael, Sarah, Pogie and Pam were seated with Pam Mailer and The Boss, James Parrot, in Marsden's personal Airfloat transporter with the refugees, the armed support group was in the second transporter.

At that moment Gene Control helimoths loomed over the treetops, "Look!" Pogie shouted, "They're going to kill us!" He thought the transporters would be helpless against the superior strength of Gene Control. In lessons at school in the Dome, the superiority of Gene Control's advanced technology had been impressed upon them by every teacher! Fortunately for the refugees—this was wrong! A clear transparent bubble was sent sailing through the air towards each of the four Helimoths, each increasing in size as it flew. In seconds, each helimoth was surrounded by these innocuous looking bubbles—each attached to one of the transporters.

"Fire!" Shouted the captain of the leading helimoth. The Crews fired as instructed. Unfortunately, the missiles could not penetrate the bubbles, and zoomed around inside them causing mayhem—and completely destroying the vehicles they surrounded and all the people inside!

"Well!" Marsden surveyed everyone in the Airfloat, "If everyone's fit, I think we can take off for Outside! There doesn't appear to be anyone left to do us harm or who needs rescuing!" Marsden's Airfloat was first to take off, followed swiftly by the second. "Take a last look at your beach home everyone!" Called Marsden. The Airfloats circled the beach. Pogie stared down at the beach in amazement, "Wait a minute! There's a man waving to us on the beach!" he pointed through the window. It was Buck, "Take me with you!" he shouted. No-one could hear what he said, but Buck's wishes were obvious. "Pick him up with the Anti-grav!" Marsden called to the Pilot. The Airfloat flew lower to hover over Buck. In the bushes, Jack took aim. Just as Buck was sucked into the air there was a hissing sound as the beam from Jack's laser shot forth—and Buck screamed in pain. The ray had burned his leg—but at least he lived to see another day—Outside.

Watching from the shelter of the trees, Jack Baillie, HCA was beside himself with rage and frustration—but he was helpless to do anything about it. Not only were the helimoths destroyed, but the staff also had been completely annihilated. Another thing! How was he to get back to Gene Control? It was going to be along walk!

The medics were dealing with Buck's injury and the Airfloats soared into the air. The Boss stood up and shouted, "We're safe! We're Safe!" All the refugees punched the air and yelled, "Hoorah!" The Boss turned to Marsden, and shook his hand, "Thank you Mr. Marsden! Thank you, on behalf of myself and all these people who have been hunted and shot at for so many years. I think I speak for everyone, when I say that you will not regret taking us in—we shall work hard in return for all the things you have promised us." Everyone cheered again.

"You are welcome," said Marsden, "There is just one thing we have forgotten—had it not been for the ingenuity and skill of these four young people you would probably never been rescued! I promise you—they shall be suitably rewarded when we get back to base." The Boss held up his arms and shouted, "Three cheers for our rescuers!"

As the transporters took off for Outside and freedom, the cheers rang out, "HIP! HIP! HOORAH! HIP! HIP! HOORAH! HIP! HIP! HOORAH!"

MAIN CHARACTERS

Katy, Ian, Michael and Sarah Stone.
Jaimie, Tom, Pogie and Pam Mailer
Buttle, the Stone's servant and reconnaissance Robot.
Jim Speke Minister for Subject Control.
John Dickson (Jack), Head of Combined Affairs
Peter Marsden from Outside Rehab.
Andrea Stevens, Katy's Mother.
The Boss
Refugees from gene Control

CPSIA information can be obtained at www.ICGtesting.com
Printed in the USA
LVOW040034100113

315128LV00004B/271/P